SCARS OF THE SOUL

"The weaknesses in the flesh
are the scars of the soul!"

Edgar Cayce

SCARS OF THE SOUL

Holistic Healing
in the Edgar Cayce Readings

by Mary Ann Woodward

Foreword by C. Norman Shealy, M.D., Ph.D.

Afterword by Michael James, Ph.D.

BRINDABELLA BOOKS

Columbus, Ohio — Fair Grove, Missouri

The author wishes to express her thanks to W.H. Church
for his editorial assistance in the preparation
of the final manuscript.

SCARS OF THE SOUL

ISBN 0-89804-903-2

TABLE OF CONTENTS

A NOTE TO THE READER

Neither the author of this book nor the Edgar Cayce Foundation, through whose kind permission various excerpts from the Edgar Cayce readings appear in the following pages, claims to offer or present the information psychically given through Edgar Cayce in clairvoyant trance state as prescription for the treatment of diseases.

Inasmuch as the Edgar Cayce readings were given to certain individuals in response to specific situations and conditions presented at the time, the psychic information often varied from one individual to the next in respect to similar or identical disease patterns, presumably due to biochemical differences or other factors. Consequently, application of medical information found in the Edgar Cayce readings should be undertaken only under supervision of a qualified physician.

All excerpts from the Edgar Cayce readings appearing in this book are identified by specific case number. The interested reader may examine any individual reading in detail at the A.R.E. Library, Virginia Beach, Virginia, where a complete file of the readings is maintained for the benefit of independent researchers as well as members of the Association for Research and Enlightenment, Inc.

SCARS OF THE SOUL

FOREWORD

by C. Norman Shealy, M.D., Ph.D.

Like most people, I knew very little about Edgar Cayce and the readings he did—let alone the idea of karma—until I had a chance to hear about the work of this great psychic first hand. This opportunity arose in August of 1972, when I attended my first conference sponsored by the Association for Research and Enlightenment—the group Cayce founded many years ago. That week had a powerful impact on me, opening up many new possibilities, giving me many peak experiences, and encouraging me to start looking into the possibility of using clairvoyant diagnosis as a healing tool.

It was at this conference that I met Mary Ann Woodward, who has become a dear friend. Mary Ann knew Cayce and was the subject of several of his readings, which helped her shape her life. From this contact, Mary Ann developed a lifelong interest in the Cayce material in general—and in the subjects of reincarnation, karma, and holistic healing in specific. She is the author of *Edgar Cayce's Story of Karma*, which has been in print since 1971, and has now compiled a sequel to that book,

Scars of the Soul, in which she looks at the relation between the principle of karma and physical health.

Throughout his life, Cayce gave almost 15,000 psychic readings on a wide variety of topics. Many dealt with specific health problems—usually health problems which had been designated as incurable by those physicians who had already been consulted. But others dealt with such arcane subjects as reincarnation, prehistoric human civilizations, and spiritual growth. Forty years after his death, we are still trying to grasp the full significance of the body of insight he left behind.

Scars of the Soul is an important new contribution to the Edgar Cayce legacy. In many ways, Cayce played an integral part in the emergence of holistic health, insisting throughout his readings that physical ailments should not be seen just as physical problems, but as problems of the whole person. To cure the whole problem, therefore, we must not just treat the physical symptoms, but also the emotional and mental weaknesses which have contributed to or caused the physical illness.

This idea alone was controversial enough in Cayce's time—and still is, for that matter, although great strides are being made in establishing holistic medicine as part of the total health picture. But Cayce added another aspect as well—the idea that many of the severe physical problems which plague us have roots in *acts and attitudes of earlier lives!*

When the sleeping Cayce first proposed the idea of reincarnation, it was a concept the waking Cayce could not accept. Having been brought up in a fundamentalist Christian family, Cayce was not at all inclined to believe in such a foreign proposition. Yet as he came to trust in the accuracy of the readings he gave while in trance, he gradually understood the basis of reincarnation and karma—and how they help us comprehend the seemingly incomprehensible aspects of human life.

Reincarnation is the simple concept that each human soul finds expression on earth through a long series of different personalities. Through each personality, the soul grows in its understanding and capacity for effective self-expression, even though most of these personalities are unaware of the higher nature of the soul—and likewise unaware of their connections to one another.

Karma is a principle which is often linked to reincarnation. It is usually referred to as the law of cause and effect, but strictly speaking, it is just one aspect of cause and effect, dealing with reactiveness. Karma holds, with Newton, that for every action there is a corresponding reaction. In human activity, this reaction may occur in the same lifetime—what Mary Ann refers to as "cash karma"—or it may be delayed and not appear in full force until some subsequent lifetime.

Karma is one of the most obvious aspects of human behavior. We reap what we sow, either good or bad. And proof of karma is available to us almost every day, if we are alert to it. Last winter, for example, my wife and I were driving on an icy, fog-bound road, carefully going only ten to twenty-five miles per hour, as conditions permitted. Suddenly, another car passed us going at least fifty miles per hour—but not for long, because as the driver accelerated in front of us, his car skidded across the road and plowed down a steep embankment. The karma of going fifty miles per hour under such adverse conditions is usually immediate and dramatic—you lose control of your car and end up wrecking it.

Other examples are just as obvious: if you drink too much alcohol, you wind up with a hangover; if you eat too much food, you become obese; if you fail to practice sensible hygiene, you will probably end up becoming ill. And examples of karmic reaction can also be found at emotional and mental levels, and in our experiences with others. Parents who ignore their children as they are growing up are often forced to deal with difficult and painful situations when the children reach adolescence and adulthood—problems of rebellion, drugs, and even criminal behavior. People who habitually treat others rudely will begin to find that they are being treated inconsiderately in return. For some people, the Golden Rule—"treat others as you would have them treat you"—ought to be amended by adding, "or they will get even with you!" They might then begin to see that this is not just an abstract moral injunction, but actually an expression of a dynamic principle of living. Whatever we do produces a reaction. If we act wisely, life will cooperate with us. If we act selfishly, life will restrict us. It is not that life is getting even with us, or punishing us. On the contrary: by the choices we make, we write the ticket for our future.

Part of the ticket we write, of course, includes the nature of our physical health. Yet many of us careen through life like the fellow who was driving fifty miles per hour on an icy highway—ignoring the issue of sound health until something goes wrong. Then we go to the doctor and expect him or her to make us well—without any involvement of our own. We certainly do not expect the doctor to tell us that we are the ones who caused our illness and that we need to stop being so angry toward life and learn to be more compassionate and tolerant! Yet this is often exactly what we do need to be told.

Edgar Cayce laid a groundwork for the holistic health movement during his career—and there were some health professionals who began working even then to explore the larger implications of the readings he gave. But it was not until the 1970's that a *movement* toward holistic concepts began to take shape—embracing not just the Cayce material but many other holistic ideas and traditions as well. A holistic perspective of health begins with the recognition that *each* individual has personal responsibility for his or her thoughts and actions. It is the whole person which is healthy or ill, not just the physical body—the whole person being an integrated system of body, emotions, mind, spirit, and lifestyle, plus the way in which he or she interacts with his or her environment. If an individual fails to exercise his or her responsibility for healthiness in any significant way—through destructive personal habits, through intense self-centeredness, by eating an unbalanced diet, or through uncontrolled fear or anger—then it is only a matter of time before ill health creates serious problems. It is inevitable because ill health is the obvious reaction to such a failure.

Edgar Cayce pointed out such connections over and over again in his health readings. But it is easy to gloss over such observations and not pay much attention to them—and even many people in the holistic health movement have not explored the karmic nature of illness as much as they should. *Scars of the Soul* takes a significant step in rectifying this problem. In case after case drawn from the Cayce readings, Mary Ann shows the relation between illness and earlier behavior—for cancer, for heart disease, for diabetes, for arthritis, for strokes, for allergies, and for many other classifications of illness.

In most cases, the antecedents which Cayce dwells on come from earlier lives. In part, this is because Cayce used the term "karma" a little differently than the textbook definition of it, to refer exclusively to patterns from earlier lives. But more importantly, it is because Cayce was trying to present a genuine holistic picture of each individual's condition. He was endeavoring to show that we are not just our physical body, or even our emotions and mind. We are much, much more than this. We are spirit in incarnation, and as such, our present experience is based on a lengthy history of earlier experience. If our present day illnesses and deficiencies have any meaning at all, they must be understood—and treated—in this larger context.

It is easy to see, after all, that lung cancer will tend to develop in a lifelong smoker more easily than in a nonsmoker—but this does not explain the fact that most lifelong smokers do not develop cancer at all. Smoking certainly contributes to the possibility of lung cancer, but to be fair, we must realize that it is not the only cause. If it were, all smokers would develop lung cancer. And so, there must be other contributing causes as well.

Edgar Cayce makes it very clear that there are—and they are to be found in the realm of our attitudes, thoughts, habits, and acts—the way we have treated others, the way we have behaved, and the good and the bad we have done. If we have been honest, generous, joyful, kind, and creative, we have written a ticket that opens up good health at all levels—healthiness in mind, emotions, the physical body, and opportunities. But if we have been selfish, mean, critical, materialistic, and pessimistic, we have written a different kind of ticket—a ticket which weakens the force of healthiness at every level. If the latter is true, then smoking may well be enough to trigger lung cancer or some other disease. But just "kicking the habit" of smoking will not be enough to generate good health—we must also kick the bad habit of being selfish, mean, critical, or a grouch.

It is important to note, in this context, that Cayce often stated that illnesses were *partially* karmic—that part of their roots came from earlier lives, but part of the problem can also be traced to present conditions. Illness, in other words, is the result of *total* stress. Genetic, environmental, physical, mental, emotional, spiritual, and karmic conditions are all involved—and must be treated. This is a true holistic perspective.

The ideas in *Scars of the Soul* are important to all of us, whether we are a health professional or just a person interested in health, whether we accept psychic realities or scoff at them. They will stretch our preconceived ideas of what health and illness are—and what must be done to create genuine healthiness. In reading this book, try to look for the universal principles of right and wrong. In an age when Americans are examining and renewing moral commitments, the Cayce philosophy deserves careful study.

Also keep in mind that this book is not a guide to intellectual understanding as much as it is a practical guide to living. Too many people seek only understanding, not wisdom; they read in order to add to their knowledge, rather than using this new knowledge to transform themselves. In her final chapter, Mary Ann presents many ideas for using meditation to begin work on the transformation of karmic patterns, based on the Edgar Cayce readings. By necessity, these comments are introductory in nature. For those who are inspired to discover more about the use of both prayer and meditation to transform karmic patterns and promote healing, I would recommend further reading in the Cayce material. In addition, I would highly recommend the writings of Dr. Robert R. Leichtman and Carl Japikse. Their book, *Active Meditation: The Western Tradition*, is an encyclopedic treatment of meditation—a true authority in the field of spiritual growth.

One final note: many people find the language used by Cayce in his readings cumbersome and even archaic. It is helpful to keep in mind that these readings were performed in a trance state very similar to the mediumistic type of trance. The sleeping Cayce did not use the same language as the waking Cayce. Yet the message is clear even when the language is not. Taking the time to reread hard-to-understand comments several times will pay off with rich rewards of new insight and awareness.

There are also occasional references in the text that follows to esoteric facts which may seem strange to people reading about Cayce for the first time—references to past lives in Atlantis, comments on astrology, and so on. For those who would like to read more about these aspects of the Cayce readings, I would recommend exploring other books in the Cayce legacy.

Dr. Shealy is the president of Holos Institutes of Health; the founding president of the American Holistic Medical Association; founder and director of the Shealy Pain and Health Rehabilitation Center and Institute, and the author of Ninety Days to Self-Health, Speedy Gourmet, The Pain Game, *and* Occult Medicine Can Save Your Life, *as well as co-author with his wife Mary-Charlotte of* To Parent or Not?

AUTHOR'S NOTE

From a scientific perspective, the case for reincarnation is still in dispute. All of the evidence, to date, can only be regarded as "circumstantial," if viewed in purely scientific terms. Yet, much of the evidence being gathered today is of a truly impressive and convincing nature. Many find it persuasive.

We know that man cannot even prove the existence of God, in acceptable philosophical terms. Yet, most people unhesitatingly believe in Him, on the basis of intuitively perceived evidence, which the non-believers term "blind faith." Similarly, many intelligent people today are able to sense the truth underlying the age-old doctrine of reincarnation—including the concept of karma, which is a pivotal aspect of that doctrine. They are at least willing to accept such ideas *conditionally,* on the basis of circumstantial data that is increasingly hard to refute.

While such ancient beliefs are only now becoming "respectable" in modern Western society, they have long been accepted tenets of Eastern philosophy and religious thought. And at least it can be argued that the doctrine of rebirth is both logical and sensible. How else can one explain the inequities of physical, mental or spiritual development with which we are born? Moreover, if there were only one lifetime allotted to us, the varied material environments and conditions in which we are placed would have to appear unjust and inexplicable to some, who long to believe in a just and loving God, or Creator. And how, within the span of a single lifetime, could we ever hope to achieve that goal of perfection we are all enjoined to strive for?

The concept of karma provides a logical explanation for many of our physical ailments and defects. Perhaps we could more readily accept, and would no longer resent, our bodily diseases and imperfections if we understood that these conditions, or "weaknesses in the flesh," were self-imposed by the Higher Self so that the soul could learn a needed lesson and thereby free itself of previously committed errors.

I believe that not only does karma explain the various physical problems with which one is born, but that a recognition of karmic law makes our problems more tolerable. When we can accept the notion that we are responsible for our present state, we are well on the way toward overcoming its limitations.

This book has been prepared with the hope and prayer that its philosophy will ease human burdens and turn our thoughts to a loving Father-Mother God, who is not punishing us but teaching us. For we are in truth our own jailors and are meting out to ourselves our own punishment. Perhaps it is better to say, as Edgar Cayce did, that in the weaknesses of the flesh we are encountering the scars of the soul.

To erase these scars, Edgar Cayce pioneered the concept of holistic healing, in which the healer attempts to harmonize the three essential aspects of man's being—body, mind and soul.

The growing popularity of holistic medicine today is not surprising. Its underlying logic is all too obvious. One only wonders that it was not recognized sooner. Instead, physicians for too long have contented themselves with the treatment of mere symptoms, ignoring the root causes of disease. But perhaps the difficulty can be traced to a philosophical dilemma: for, basic to the principles of holistic healing as presented by Cayce, is an implicit acknowledgment and acceptance of the idea of karma. And this, in turn, involves a willingness to consider the doctrine of reincarnation. Fortunately, there has been some significant progress in this direction in recent years, through the pioneering research work of such people as Drs. Elisabeth Kubler-Ross, Morris Netherton, and others, demonstrating the continuity of life.

Their findings, I believe, are gradually pointing the way to a synthesis yet to come, which will harmonize the traditional belief systems of East and West. They are perhaps more similar than we have ever imagined. And how could it be otherwise, really? For it is written: "The Lord thy God is One!"

This book, based on the principles of holistic healing as set forth in the physical readings given by Edgar Cayce half a century ago, will, I trust, make the reader more aware of that Oneness.

Mary Ann Woodward

CHAPTER ONE

WHAT IS PHYSICAL KARMA?

There are many types of karma. A nation, for example, accrues karma of a good or bad nature, depending upon the collective actions of its citizenry and its government; and what is sown must ultimately be reaped in a future cycle of the nation's history. The same may be said of a city, of a group, or of any type of organization. At a more personal level, karma pertains to consequential conditions or events in the life of the individual, stemming from his or her past relationships, thoughts and actions.

What, then, is *physical* karma? It may be described as a manifestation of karmic law taking place at a visible or physical level within the human body.

Let us review our definitions of karma. Karma is usually thought of—although not quite accurately—as the law of cause and effect:

Cause and effect to many are the same as karma. Yet, [that which is] karmic is that brought over, while cause

19.

and effect may exist in the one material experience only.

(2981-2)

More specifically, karma is a term used in a philosophical sense to describe conditions or events occurring in the present as a consequence of thoughts and actions in the past. The Sanskrit meaning encompasses both action and reaction; and Karma Yoga, which is a Hindu discipline, is based on the concept of "work," or the labor of the soul seeking to attain union with God through service to man.

Edgar Cayce said karma was "meeting self":

For as has so oft been given, 'As ye sow, so may ye reap.'
Or each soul, entity, is constantly meeting itself. (1506-1)

Karma is, then, that that has been in the past builded as *indifference* to that *known* to be right! (257-78)

God has not willed that any soul should perish. In order to blot out the past and create "good karma" now, one entity was told:

Lose self in the consciousness of the *indwelling* of the Creative Force, in that channel as has been prepared for the escape of the sons *and* daughters of men, through the *Son* of man! This is the escape, and what is to be done about it! Lose self; make His Will one with *thy* will.

(275-23)

The Law of Grace, or divine forgiveness, is thus implemented.

According to Cayce, there must be a time-lag of at least one earth life in order to consider a condition "karmic," although the error which caused the condition often goes back many lifetimes.

Many physical conditions appear inexplicable to us, particularly when they are medically incurable and a loved one is suffering. According to the Edgar Cayce readings, each person is responsible for the circumstances in which he finds himself. He is not the innocent victim of his environment, as we are inclined to suppose, but is simply brought into a situation where he is best able to "meet self."

What ye sow, ye reap. Apparently there are often experiences in which individuals reap that which they have not sown, but this is only the short self-vision of the entity or the one analyzing and studying purposes or ideals in relationships to those particular individuals.   (2528-3)

Dr. William A. McGarey, Medical Director of the A.R.E. Clinic and Director of the Medical Research Division of the Edgar Cayce Foundation, says: "I've come to the conclusion that most of the serious, long-term, degenerative diseases are karmic in their nature.   Things like Parkinson's Disease, Rheumatoid Arthritis, Amyotrophic Lateral Sclerosis, Muscular Dystrophy...and the like.   There are seemingly antagonistic viewpoints expressed both in the world of literature, the Bible and in the readings, about the reversibility potential in people experiencing these diseases."

Under the light of spiritual law, however, it becomes apparent that the healing potential of the Christ pattern is ever-present.   For, to quote case 3744-1, "There are in truth no *incurable* conditions."   The divinity that shapes our ends is within ourselves.   How well do we wish to be?   The readings point out, very clearly:

That there is within self all healing that may be accomplished for the body. For, all healing must come from the Divine. For who healeth thy diseases? The source of the Universal supply. As the attitude, then, of self, how well do you wish to be? How well are ye willing to cooperate, coordinate with the Divine influences which may work in and through thee, by stimulating the centers which have been latent with nature's activities? For, all of these forces must come from the one source, and the applications are merely to stimulate the atoms of the body. For each cell is as a representative of a universe in itself. Then what would ye do with thy abilities? As ye give to others, not hating them, to know more of the Universal Forces, so may ye have the more, for, God is Love.   (4021-1)

Here, again, we find Edgar Cayce pointing out, in two separate cases, the need for the individual to assume a responsible role if it would meet and overcome self:

We find these conditions may be materially aided. As to how far the corrections may go will depend upon the consistency and persistence of the body as it makes administrations for correcting the disturbance. Thus the beginning must be in the mental attitude of the body-mind. There must be kept a creative, constructive attitude, and not the condemning or faultfinding of others—which has been a portion of the karmic forces being met in self.
                    (3563-1)

As each soul enters this material plane, it is to meet or to give those lessons or truths that others, too, may gain the more knowledge of the purpose for which each soul enters.   (3645-1)

In the end, we have to accept this truth: all that a man achieves, or fails to achieve, lies within himself; for his success or failure is the direct outcome of his own thoughts and actions, reflecting the degree of spiritual attunement, or at-one-ment, he has reached.

Whereas Dr. McGarey has concluded, with appropriate medical caution, that "*most* of the serious, long-term, degenerative diseases are karmic in nature," the Cayce readings appear to be more all-inclusive on this point. In addition to such maladies as epilepsy, diabetes, tuberculosis, cancer, psoriasis or alcoholism, where the karmic link can sometimes be quite evident, we find in the readings that even an "accident" may be of karmic origin. It would seem, in the ultimate analysis, that any of our ills is somehow contingent upon our own thoughts and actions, and must be seen against a karmic backdrop. For our attitudes and emotions, our resentments, our loves and hates may have persisted from a previous incarnation, causing psychological or psychosomatic problems which finally culminate in some serious illness or accident, or at least perpetuate an imaginary ailment. Today many physical conditions are being recognized as psychological or psychosomatic in origin and are being treated on a mental level. The condition is usually alleviated when the sufferer recognizes his error and begins to cope with the problem at an inner level.

An illness or physical discomfort of some sort, such as a headache or indigestion, often appears after or during an emotional upset. Many people find that a cold follows a fit of anger or prolonged distress. Not that righteous indignation is not sometimes justified; but temper tantrums are a disaster, affecting others as well as self, for they inevitably result in some form of acute physical discomfort and strained relationships that are hurtful all around. Also, inflamed or irritated skin conditions frequently occur in conjunction with moods of irritation or distress. And we all know that our pain in the neck can come from someone being, quite literally, a "pain in the neck" to us—for nervous disorders readily appear as a result of some deep-seated annoyance we have failed to counteract. Indeed, negative attitudes and emotions boomerang so quickly that we could call them "cash karma"! For we do pay our debt to our higher self almost instantly, in certain situations, and should be grateful to have the lessons of our backslidings brought home to us so swiftly. On the other hand, a soul-searching analysis may reveal that these negative responses of ours are actually the sign of deep-seated personality problems, which result from unconstructive attitudes and emotions we have habitually indulged in throughout several earth lives or more. So we have brought them over with us into the present life. Then, each of us needs to ask of ourself: Do I wish to take this undesirable trait with me into my next life, as well, or will I overcome it *now*?

One way to identify a karmic problem or condition without extensive self-analysis, of course, is through a qualified psychic source such as Edgar Cayce, who can "give a reading" that will reveal to us our karmic patterns, as it were. I was fortunate enough to have such a reading from Mr. Cayce, and it aided me greatly in "meeting self" during the subsequent years of my life. But since the average individual is not apt to encounter a psychic with the unusual talents that were exhibited by the late Edgar Cayce, a more practical approach is to ask of ourselves certain questions which will enable us to pinpoint or identify the karmic roots from which our ills arise.

The first question, whether pertaining to self or another: Was the affliction evident from birth? Then ask: Is it a defect (such as a malformed limb, for example) or a dis-ease? If not from birth, or congenital, has it been of relatively long duration? Does it appear to respond readily to treatment? Or is the condition a malfunction resisting any treatment? Is the healing process, if occurring, abnormally slow or beset with relapses? At least one or more of these characteristics marked the multitude of physical conditions or ills which Edgar Cayce identified as karmic. We could also ask: What seemingly trivial or unrelated incident—a minor fall or accident, perhaps—may have preceded the onset of a chronic dis-ease or dysfunction? For, identifying the trigger-point of a karmic condition, although it may at first appear to be unrelated, may provide a valuable clue to meeting self and overcoming the condition.

CHAPTER TWO

WHAT CAUSES PHYSICAL KARMA?

What causes physical karma? This is a very complicated question, as some sort of balancing of forces is manifesting. Moreover, it may manifest on all three levels—physical, mental and spiritual. Edgar Cayce said we do something to start it, and then we meet it in the circulation. This apparently can go on for centuries unless we do something to correct the underlying error or sin.

Reading 275-19 tells us that "the weaknesses in the *flesh* are the scars of the soul." Since we bring the condition or problem with us when we are born, the spiritual errors of former lives lead the soul to choose a new body which will be genetically weak in those areas in which the soul needs to acquire a lesson. The constitution of this new body is inherited from the parents, who supply the genes and chromosomes which determine the neurological, musculoskeletal, vascular, biochemical, immunological and glandular systems.

The *New York Times* of August 30, 1978, offers a scientific explanation of the relationship of genes to birth defects:

ISOLATING THE GENE

Also for the first time last week, doctors from Harvard, Yale and the Haceteppi University in Turkey announced the diagnosis of a fetal defect by isolation and identification of a single gene of the estimated three to four million in a human cell. The gene identified directs production of hemoglobin, the iron compound that carries oxygen in the blood.

In principle, doctors can now determine, by sampling cells from the fluid around the human fetus for the presence or absence of that gene, whether the fetus suffers from certain debilitating and sometimes fatal forms of anemia. Detection previously required a sample of fetal blood, which is risky to take. These anemias are rare, but researchers have predicted that within a few years they will be able to examine for more common genetic diseases, such as cystic fibrosis.

It is provocative to compare this idea with the Cayce readings, which state that defects often involve a lesson for the parents as well as the child.

The importance of the glandular system and its relationship to the physical and spiritual development of an entity is indicated in this excerpt from one of the Cayce readings:

> This spiritual contact is through the glandular forces of creative energies: not encased only within the...gland of reproduction, for this is ever—so long as life exists—in contact with the brain cells through which there is the constant reaction through the pineal. (263-13)

Physically, the immunological system may be one of the most important. It determines our ability to resist certain diseases. The endocrine glands are the physical expression of the chakras or spiritual centers of the etheric body. As Cayce said in case 281-38: "For this is the system whereby or in which dispositions, characters, natures and races all have their source." The hormones produced by these glands affect all the other systems. We are told:

> Karmic influences are more of the spiritual than of an earth's experience, for what we create in the earth we meet in the earth—and what we create in the realm through spiritual forces we meet there! And getting outside of the realm of the material does not mean necessarily angelic, or angelic influences!   (314-1)

So the glandular system is of utmost importance karmically. With this great interplay of forces in the new body we can see that the same act does not necessarily produce the same physical effect.

A close relationship between the endocrine system and the emotions was indicated in this excerpt:

> For, as has been indicated in some manners, some activities, there is an activity within the system produced by anger, fear, mirth, joy, or any of those active forces, that produces through the glandular secretion those activities that flow into the whole of the system. Such an activity then is of this endocrine system, and only has been observed in very remote manners.   (281-38)

The glandular system's importance is also indicated by the fact that many karmic conditions appear first at adolescence, when the glandular system becomes most noticeably active. Thus we see that there are direct and indirect causes of karmic maladies. There is the soul within, and the spiritual problem which must be worked out or faced at some time. Then there is the direct or visible cause such as a birth defect or other bodily condition triggered by some physical means, such as an accident, stress, an emotional upset or a disease, perhaps.

Edgar Cayce said:

All illness comes from sin. This everyone must take whether they like it or not; it comes from sin—whether it be of body, of mind, or of soul. (3174-1)

Man walked away from his Maker and became very self-centered:

As man's concept came to that point wherein man walked not after the ways of the Spirit but after the desires of the flesh, *sin* entered—that is, away from the Face of the Maker. (900-227)

Know ye not that it was selfishness that separated the souls from the spirit of life and light? Then only in the divine love do ye have the opportunity to become to thy fellow man a saving grace, a mercy, yea, even a savior.
(987-4)

It is difficult to accept that illness is sin; but sin, as the theologians say, is really separation from God. If we were at all times attuned to God or Creative Forces, obeying His laws, doing His will, we would not suffer from any malady. As it is stated in Exodus 15:26: "If thou wilt diligently hearken to the voice of the Lord thy God, and wilt do that which is right in His sight, and wilt give ear to His commandments, and keep all His statutes, I will put none of these diseases upon thee, which I have brought upon the Egyptians: for I *am* the Lord that healeth thee."

The relation of sin and disease was explained further, in this reading:

Disease arises from, first, dis-ease—as a normalcy that *is* existent and yet becomes unbalanced. Disease is, or dis-ease is, a state at variance to the ideal or first cause or first principle. Then, in its final analysis, disease might be called sin. It is necessary to keep a balance.

And those who are in a material world are naturally subject to, and in contact with, sin. Thus the individual entity or soul-entity is to meet, to come in contact with, to overcome, to subdue same. For, what is the first premise? 'Be fruitful, multiply, but *subdue* the earth.' Then, dis-ease is of the earth—earthy. (2533-3)

Many times Edgar Cayce told people that "the only sin of man is *selfishness!*" Actually, when we list the so-called seven deadly sins—envy, pride, covetousness, gluttony, sloth, lust and anger—we can see that the sinner, in each instance, is thinking only of self.

On the material level, the body is controlled primarily by emotions and attitudes. Whenever some dis-ease or malady occurs, there is a conflict in evidence between the mental and soul forces. We have been given the gift of free will so that we might develop to become companions and co-creators with God. But man, from the very beginning, chose to rebel against God's laws and His will, so that conflict, confusion and dis-ease have resulted rather than harmony and dominion.

In order to overcome the karmic consequences he has brought about, man must seek and find the inner causes and correct them through mental and spiritual effort. For the *real* cause of any bodily disturbance is always on a level above the physical self; and the dis-ease or other problem forces the individual to seek God by turning within and setting aright his errors.

Our attitudes and emotions produce reactions which cause many of our problems and diseases. In fact, there are clear patterns which inevitably result from negative emotions and attitudes. Edgar Cayce said no one can hate his neighbor and not have stomach or liver trouble! No one can be jealous and allow the anger of same, and not have upset digestion or heart disorder. "These should be warnings," he said in case 2-14, "for every human: madness [anger] is certainly poison to the system."

We are reminded of the words of Paul: "Be angry, but do not sin; do not let the sun go down on your anger, and give no opportunity to the devil." (Ephesians 4:26-27)

Anger, resentment, revenge, and all such forms of un-tempered wrath serve to cloud our judgment. Entertaining violent emotions may give some momentary pleasure and relief but is disastrous in the long run. Nothing seems to promise us so much as "sweet revenge," but repays us so little! And consider our numerous prejudices, which stick to us like burrs: so easy to pick up, so hard to drop. It is no wonder, then, that in quite a number of the readings given by Edgar Cayce the sufferer was admonished to change his attitude and outlook as a necessary precondition to physical improvement. So, we do indeed learn through pain and suffering. These handmaidens of karma serve to convert the soul. After all, if we are prone to make mistakes, it is well that we should learn from them!

This next excerpt from one of the readings offers a beautiful explanation of the process by which a physical weakness develops in the body, through the breaking of natural or spiritual laws:

Are all physical weaknesses and ailments caused primarily from breaking of spiritual laws, instead of just physical or natural laws as we know them?

Rather the combination of each; as in the physical forces they are the activities from those things just indicated as to how color comes into—or tone comes into—its physical existence from the spiritualization of sound, or spiritualization of the vibrations that are set up by elementals, or by forces in same. So with the activities in the body. These come from the first urge—which is the meeting of the union of forces that create, as the beginning of inception, and those elements then that enter in by the feeding, when it begins with the changes of same, make for certain indications; and the functioning of glands, as are indicated, that make for the height or that make for color, or as to make for the functioning of various conditions. Then, it's a combination of these. Yet, as has been indicated, *always* will it be found that the *attitude* of the mental forces of a body finds its inception in those things that come into growth; for what we think and what we eat—combined together—make what we *are*, physically and mentally. (288-38)

It would be more interesting and possibly more helpful in understanding the following cases, based on what were termed "physical" readings by Edgar Cayce, if the individuals concerned had also received "life" readings, giving background data on their prior lives in the earth and the karmic residue from those earlier experiences in this plane.

The case of a woman bears this out:

Now we find there are abnormal conditions with this body. These are hidden in a manner, and are an interesting study from psychological and pathological conditions as come about in the variation of the effects as are produced by conditions that have not been easily understood, and dissension and discussion has often arisen as respecting that as produces same. *Most* interesting for this body would have been the experiences as produced same in the *entity's* experience. We deal with those in the present.

(5578-1)

A discourse from reading 2533-6, on longevity, is given here as it throws much light on what produces physical conditions or weaknesses; therefore, it sheds light equally on the physical manifesting of karma:

In giving a discourse upon how this entity may extend the life expectancy, with a body-mind activity in keeping with the conditions to which the entity may hope to attain—to be sure each entity, each soul, is in many respects a law unto itself; especially as related to the activities and the diets that would extend or impel life expectancy.

Thus, that which might be applicable in the experience of the entity as may be indicated here, should *not* be forced upon, or even considered for others; unless their *own* condition is in that state of being parallel with this individual entity.

To be sure—as indicated in the study by the entity—those things that have to do with body, mind and activities of a body, are the result in a physical manner from those conditions which existed in the experience of their parents.

For, as is determined, and as is the fact, there *are* circumstances and conditions which arise in the genealogical reactions that extend, as indicated in the law, 'unto the third and fourth generation.'

These, then, are tendencies, inclinations as may arise in bodies; provided such bodies are not aware of such, or if measures are not taken to correct such weaknesses or tendencies as may be found to be a part of the physical experience of an entity.

Also there are those inclinations, those urges, those experiences, that will be a part of the mental and the spiritual entity, from that the entity did in the earthly sojourns as related to the law pertaining to the moral, spiritual and material aspects of an entity's consciousness.

But as related to this entity, and how this entity may apply in its own individual experience the truth, the law, the knowledge of interpretation of those activities of a physical-material nature, of dietetics and the like.

As we have indicated for the body, there are certain tendencies, certain weaknesses that are present in the body. They are not *diseases*—these are rather dis-eases, when certain stresses or strains are brought to bear in the mental, in the spiritual and physical experience of the entity.

Urges arise, then, not only from what one eats but from what one thinks; and from what one does about what one thinks and eats! As well as what one digests mentally and spiritually!

The weaknesses that exist in this particular body are a projection of those conditions which existed in the present grandfather of the entity, in an experience in the earth; and has to do with those elements bearing upon the hormones of the blood force itself. And in the body [2533], it exhibits as a tendency.

To eradicate, to eliminate such from the body, is to be interpreted from that given in the beginning: 'Be ye fruitful, multiply, but *subdue* the tendencies, the inclinations, 'the earth.' For, in manifestation in the earth of spiritual and mental forces, it partakes of the earth. And the earth is earthy, as it changes, as it is in constant change.

And that which bespeaks of longevity in a body bespeaks of each cell, each atomic structure, each of the corpuscles being able to reproduce itself *without* those tendencies or inclinations of racial or environmental conditions, but as one purified or cleansed for that continuity of experience within itself.

Knowing these tendencies, these weaknesses, does not then indicate that there are those bugaboos continually before the entity. For, these are left behind when ye do that ye know to do, and leave undone those things ye must or else pay the price of neglect, over-indulgence, gratification for the moment that there may be the satisfying of an appetite or tendency as may exist in the body!

Here we find the necessity for care, for exercise, for constant checking upon the bodily activities; not daily, necessarily—but remember that the body-physical alters in its expression continually, and by the end of a cycle of seven years it has entirely replaced that which existed at the beginning of the period seven years ago.

Replaced with what? The same old tendencies multiplied, the same old inclinations doubled—or eradicated?

This depends, then, upon those activities as related to the influences or tendencies which exist. For, as may be told by any pathologist, there is no known reason why any individual entity should not live as long as it desires. And there is no death, save in thy consciousness. Because all others have died, ye expect to—and you do! These are a part of thy consciousness, in what? In the mental, in the spiritual—and the physical reacts to same.

This is the condition that exists, then, with this body; a weakness, a tendency—not a disease but a dis-ease—in the hormones of the blood plasm; that tends—with cold, congestion, overacidity, or the improper balance of foods for the plasm's reproduction—to cause in sinew, in bone, a plastic or static condition.

As far as the blood count is concerned, in numbers, in protoplasm cells, or red blood, white blood and the leucocyte, we would find few bodies better balanced than this individual entity.

As to the plasms in the nerve reflexes from brain, and the coordination of the gray and white matter—only at times do we find these show a variation.

Frustration will at times cause, to this body, a reaction that becomes rather aggravating to the body afterwards. At the moment it is too much disturbed to even know the cause of same, but it blesses itself out, or someone else, after same is passed!

This is a reflex from the hormone supply, the inability to supply in the brain circulation sufficient of the quick activity to the impulses there, under stress.

These are merely tendencies in the body.

As to the spiritual tendencies and inclinations—these may not be given. For these are choices of the soul itself.

The tendencies as to the ideal are well. As to whether ye keep same, this ye determine in thine own mind.

But ideals are not your mind—ideals are principles

acted upon *by* the mind. But remember, just as that expectancy—because your great, great, great, great grandfather died you will die too—is there, and is part of the expectancy of every cell of your body! It can be eradicated, yes. How? By that constant activity within self of expectancy that this condition does not *have* to happen to you!

That is as the spirit. And as the spirit builds, as the spirit forms in its activity in mind, the mind becomes then the builder. The mind is not spirit, it is a companion to the spirit; it builds a pattern. And this is the beginning of how self may raise that expectancy of its period of activity in the earth. And this is the beginning of thy ideal. Of what? Of that the soul should, does, will, can, must accomplish in this experience!

And by what authority? WHO, WHAT do you put in authority in thy earthly experience? In spirit, then in mind?

As to the manner of eradicating these fluctuations, these confusions—do not confuse these with that as of a 'front,' as of a defense. But merely to know that you are right, to know in activity that you are right, has paved the way for self to control any situation that may arise—whether of a mental confusion or a combination of confusions from the mental and spiritual situations.

Hence again in the mental rests upon its conception and choice of its ideal in spirit, and as to Who and What is the authority in same.

As to the physical conditions that are a part of the pathological effects in the body:

At certain periods have those tests as to acidity, albumin, the balance in chyle activity through the body, as to glandular reactions; and these give then the positive or negative flexes in the body.

Knowing the tendencies, supply in the vital energies that ye call vitamins, or elements. For, remember, while we give many combinations, there are only four elements in your body—water, salt, soda and iodine. These are the basic elements, they make all the rest! Each vitamin as a component part of an element is simply a combination of these other influences, given a name mostly for confusion to individuals, by those who would tell you what to do for a price!

In those activities, then, add—in the proper balance—that which will maintain this equilibrium. And if you set your life to be a hundred and twenty, you can live to be a hundred and twenty-one!   (2533-6)

========= CHAPTER THREE =========

EXAMPLES OF PHYSICAL KARMA

In 1971, the *Ledger-Star* of Norfolk, Virginia, reported heart disease, cancer, stroke and accidents as the four "big killers."

Today—some ten years later—the listing of the "big killers" has shifted a bit. Heart disease still comes first, then cancer, followed by accidents (plus pneumonia, as a newcomer to the list) and then diabetes, with the latter currently preceding strokes as a major cause of death.

As one generation or cycle moves on, preparing for the next, we may expect to see somewhat different patterns emerging. Society is ever in a state of flux. But although diseases and their names may shift and change with the passage of time, the fact remains that mankind has always been scourged with a number of "big killer" diseases throughout history. It is as if such major afflictions were an inescapable aspect of fleshly existence.

Are these major causes of death linked to *karmic* conditions, or patterns, which we have brought over with us from our prior lives in the earth? It is my conviction that in the ultimate analysis *all* of these "killer" diseases can be considered to have karmic origins, although it is a hypothesis that cannot be scientifically proven as yet. Environmental factors, diet and such, all may play a role, of course, which does not alter the point that the manifestation of disease is nevertheless karmic in its essence. There may even be an esoteric connection of some kind between specific diseases that gain temporary "popularity" and certain "soul clusters" that are currently reincarnating in the earth-plane; for the Edgar Cayce readings make it plain that there is a tendency for souls with a karmic linkage from the past (such as the last of the Atlanteans, for example, who shared in the responsibility for the final destruction of their fabled empire!) to reincarnate together in recurring cycles, working out their karmic indebtedness as a group. Might they not also tend to experience similar diseases, for fleshly ills?

Many of the readings Edgar Cayce gave to individuals suffering from what we have termed the "big killer" diseases told them that the error or sin, which was the inner or real cause of the present suffering, occurred long ago in another life. The individual was normally told that he needed to do an "about face" in his attitude and become more in attunement with Creative Forces, or God, if he wished to be healed.

> Thy relationships to thy fellows through the various experiences in the earth come to be then in the light of what Creative Forces would be in thy relationship to the *act itself*.
> (1436-3)

We live under grace to the exact extent that we are attuned to God. Each of the major types of disease which afflicts humanity can be seen as a message that we are not properly attuned.

Cancer

Today cancer is probably the most feared disease. The fact that it is becoming more prevalent and is usually considered

38.

incurable makes the vast majority of people fear it even more.

Today we live in what Dr. Bernard Jensen calls a "carcinogenic environment." In *Health Magic Through Chlorophyll*, he writes: "Many of these substances that are found to be carcinogenic are used on our fruits and vegetables. That is why I say we are living in a carcinogenic environment. We are living in it, drinking it, eating it."

It appears that many cancer cases are what I would call "cash karma." We have apparently brought on the illness in this life due to our environment and diet.

Cancer, at times, seems to be very prevalent in a certain family. Yet it is a disease that is not considered contagious. For example, in a Kansas family known to the writer, which included ten children, five members died of cancer. Moreover, they lived in an area we would not consider carcinogenic. We might infer that there was a common genetic weakness, inasmuch as the mother was among the five who died of cancer.

What is the disease known as cancer?

As we have indicated in other information, there are many varied kinds of cancer. Nineteen — as we find — variations or formations, externally, internally, stony, and the variations that arise from glandular or organic disturbance, or infectious forces that arise from bruises or from all the various natures from which these come; each having a variation according to that portion of the system or its cycle in which the affectation takes place.   (1246-6)

This indicates that the disturbance known as cancer can occur any place in the body and may be classified according to its location. Cells which accumulate in any organ obviously take on some or all of the characteristics of the organ; so different areas in the physical account for various types of cancerous cells. The build-up seems to occur where there is a malfunction or an accumulation of drosses. Possibly a major cause is the liver's failure to carry out its functions. The following excerpt from one of the Cayce readings throws some light on this:

As to the seat and cause of this, we find of long standing. Not exactly of a prenatal condition, but of a pre-disposition, as it were, toward the weakness in the body, and the inactivity of hepatic circulation and the throwing, as it were, of all the stress on the functioning of the lower portion of the hepatic circulation. This, as is seen, rather of the chronic nature by the character of the water as has been taken by the body, and through the slushing of the system without cleansing the system, and this then caused an unstabilization between the action of the kidneys and the liver themselves, and began with the uric acid, and this brings about that condition as exists in the present.

Then, to meet the needs—as has been given, follow out those lines as being followed; being very careful of the diet, that it does not carry those properties that cause distress to the digestive system, especially in the form of gases or any condition that will bring a taxation to the hepatic circulation in its elimination. Centralize the elimination, especially, through the capillary and lymphatic circulation, either by that of the baths or packs, and let the medicinal properties as given be not as a counter-irritant, but as active forces with those organs as are seen that cause the distress. Do that.   (70-1)

One fellow asked Cayce: "What is the origin of these cancerous tumors?" He was told: "Karma. We do something to start this and then we meet it in the circulation." Obviously, the process is very complicated and affects all vital processes. Today much of the literature on cancer refers to it as a metabolic disease. This seems to agree with this last quote. In fact, many of the so-called incurable diseases are said to be metabolic.

In certain cases, the Edgar Cayce readings recommended animated ash and violet ray, a form of ultraviolet, in the treatment of cancer. Diet also was often stressed, and there have reportedly been cures following this procedure. It is interesting to note in Maurice Finkel's book, *Fresh Hope for Cancer*, which records a number of cancer cures around the world, that treatment generally has involved a dietary regimen and a method of getting oxygen into the system. Cancer cells are anaerobic, which means that they do not require direct oxygen as other cells in the body do. In fact, oxygen seems to *destroy* cancerous cells.

Reading 2098-1 was one of the first cases for which the use of animated ash was recommended. This is a cancer case; and although the reading does not specifically identify the illness as karmic, it probably was, for the mental and spiritual attitudes were stressed.

As to the causes of these, as *we* find, from infectious forces from broken cellular tissue, as produced by those of an external nature, as well as the mental attitude that was gradually builded by the body.

As to those ministrations that are being given, we would not alter these—save as to add that which would induce a better oxidization, or releasing more oxygen; for there would be the necessary elements in same that resuscitating forces may be enlivened to that degree as to bring about a better channel through which the mental and spiritual forces may keep the equilibrium between the physical forces and that which makes for life itself in a human or material body.

These, as we find, may be added in small quantities of the animated or carbon ash, with the use of the ultra-violet with same. This, to be sure, will be found then necessary to add to those applications for a more normal carrying on of the life forces in the bloodstream itself, and lessening the stress that is being made on the portions of the body in the functioning of the organs of the circulatory system, as related both to the heart and respiratory system, as well as

41.

the organs that make for the clarification and the oxidation of used or impelling forces that are active in resuscitation of life itself in a physical body.　　　　(2098-1)

The previously cited excerpt from reading 70-1 was from a cancer case which indicated that it could be a karmic condition, for the condition was described as a "predisposition" and weakness. Furthermore, several other cancer cases were stated as being prenatal in origin. The other cancer cases reported herein are definitely identified as being karmic.

Case 3391, involving a little boy only two years of age, appears to be a clear case of karmic cancer. The child was apparently born with the condition. The parents are advised not to try too hard to hold the child in material manifestation but to attune to the spiritual, thus indicating that the underlying "lesson" is as much, or more for the parents' sake, as for the child's.

Yes. As we find, conditions are very serious. There should not be too great a stress put upon determining to hold this body in material manifestation. Not that the hope and trust in the divine is to be lessened. Rather should it be exercised the more in realizing, even with the material, what the handicaps would be. These should give rather the parents, those so close, the feeling of their interest, of their witness before the Throne of grace and mercy.

There are physical disturbances that are a part of the entity's karma. They are for lessons for those responsible for the body, if ye will accept it. If ye let it harden thee, ye miss the opportunity of knowing that He is the resurrection, He is the truth and life.

Put thy child rather at all times into the arms of Jesus.

In the physical we would apply those conditions that may aid. As developments progress, let that which is of the divine determine whether it is best in this consciousness or in the universal consciousness that it is to serve.

The sarcoma through the body is in the bloodstream. It may be kept localized by the application of Plantain Salve.

[Further direction for treatment with packs and lights was given.]

Then keep the body quiet. Keep in prayer, and let it ever be, 'Thy will, O God—Thy will be done.'

Then live it, not merely say it, but live it in the daily association with others. 'As ye would that men should do to you, do ye even so to them.'   (3991-1)

Five other cases of karmic cancer are also presented here. They are varied both as to type and suggestions for treatment. (While treatments are partially quoted here or referred to at times, no attempt is made to cover treatment as that is beyond the scope of this book. However, it is interesting to note, in passing, that the recommended treatments consisted of rather simple home remedies which included herbs, massage, lights and diet.) These five cases do bring out the spiritual aspect of the condition and the need for change in attitudes, as well as work at the spiritual level. This is a significant aspect, for the readings not designated as karmic dwell more on the physical condition and treatment. So we might deduce that these several cases, which follow here, are instances of individuals meeting a more definite lesson in their suffering, presumably because they are ready now to accept responsibility for their past actions and to experience the lesson to be learned.

The first is case 3313, from which we can gain further insights into causal factors, as well as the relationship between karma and heredity:

We find here that the body should consider more of the spiritual than the material things of life. While there may be yet much accomplished by this body, these should be the attitudes of the body. For, it is meeting itself in its own activities.

Those disturbances of the prostate glands are of the

nature that there may be added those conditions that will allay the disturbances.

The applications being made are well, but we would add the animated ash.

Then, keep the mental attitude in that way of knowing in what there is life, light and immortality. It is not all of death to die, nor all of life to live. When there is sought that peace with Him, this may be had. For His promises are sure.

When it becomes necessary for changes, these we find—with the use of such as indicated—may be delayed much time. And there will be that peace, if the trust is set in Him.

Ready for questions.

Is an operation inevitable?

This depends upon the attitude and upon the response the body makes and those general reactions in the body.

Any suggested diet for the body?

That as indicated for the body is very well.   (2911-1)

Case 3121, which follows, emphasizes "spiritual attitude first," in the approach to healing:

As we find, there are disturbing conditions. This disturbance is of a nature that by some would be called karmic.   Hence it is something the body *physically,* mentally, must meet, in its spiritual attitude first; that is: as the body may dedicate its life and its abilities to a definite service, to the Creative Forces or God, there will be healing forces brought to the body.

This requires, then, that the mental attitude be such as to not only proclaim or announce a belief in the Divine, and to promise to dedicate self to same, but the entity must *consistently* live such.   And the test, the proof of same, is long-suffering.   This does not mean suffering of self and not grumbling about it.   Rather, though you be persecuted, unkindly spoken of, taken advantage of by others, you do not attempt to fight back or to do spiteful things; that you be patient—first with self, then with others; again that you not only be passive in your relationships with others but active, being kindly, affectionate one to the other; remembering as He has said, 'Inasmuch as ye do it unto the least, ye do it unto Me.' As oft as you contribute, then, to the welfare of those less fortunate, visit the fatherless and the widows in their affliction, visit those imprisoned—rightly or wrongly—you do it to your Maker. For, TRUTH shall indeed make you free, even though you be bound in the chains of those things that have brought errors, or the result of errors, in your own experience.

This, then, is the first spiritual approach—or the attitude with which the entity would seek to administer that which is helpful, that which will be met in nature.

For, as so oft has been indicated, each entity, each soul manifesting in the earth, is the result of that the entity has been, in its use of its opportunities, in its relationship to God the Father.

In the beginning let us consider that there is the body, the mind, the soul. The soul is spirit; the mind is as gas that may have its high or low pressure, and the body of its own; but the physical is of the earth—earthy. However, the body was made, was first created, of everything that was in the earth. Hence there are those influences that will meet these tendencies in the blood supply toward that called sarcoma in its nature.

This is a form, of course, of infectious disturbance of such natures as to fasten upon a body for its own destructive forces, and cells breaking have joined—as it were—one force against another. At times the destructive forces are in excess, and thus the injured portions of the body become more and more beset with these growths in the body, and they sap the vitality.

The organs, as organs, are very good. The body-mind is

45.

good; the tempering of same is within itself capable of being used towards being a helpful influence to someone, somewhere, sometime. And the time is ever now, when the opportunity presents itself.

The blood is infected, then, with these disturbances; such that the very nature of these induces the cellular force or the red corpuscles to become involved with same. And the sufficiency or the efficacy of the leukocytes in white blood to break or block off these gradually loses ground, when there is lack of sufficient vital forces in the bloodstream to increase the number of the white blood and leukocyte force.

Hence this appears in the present to be more of a lymph involvement, but now and then the supplying of the vital energies is lacking, especially in Vitamins D and B Complex, and K and G, the body is enabled to find or fight or to supply resistances in the fluid forces of the body for energizing and giving energy and life to the body.

Most of all, pray. Let the mental attitude be considered first and foremost. Do not promise thyself, nor thy God, nor thy neighbor, that you do not fulfill.   (3121-1)

This next cancer case was given a large margin of hope. Also, there is included the unusual recommendation of a magnet passed over the "affected areas:"

As we find, conditions are such that there may be a staying of the disturbances, but these activities are of the consuming nature.

If there is the desire, there may be used the influences that we might suggest—though these will not heal, or remove causes. For, as has been indicated oft, causes may be karma. Karma is cause oft of hereditary conditions so-called. Then indeed does the soul inherit that it has builded in its experience with its fellow man in material relationships.

The conditions here may be best retarded by the use at times, about once a week, of a magnet—of sufficient strength to raise a railroad spike—this being passed over affected areas, see? This will aid in demagnetizing or producing a vibration that will destroy the active forces of the consuming of cells being enlivened by the infection itself.

Keep as normal an appetite and actions of the body as possible.

These offer the greater help here; not a cure, but a retarder; an easing.

Use the sedatives when intense pains arise. Hypnotics are preferable to narcotics.

Is an operation necessary or advisable?

More apt to lessen the longevity or length of this life's span. May be done if it is desired.

The basic cause is karmic.   (3313-1)

Another cancer victim was told:

As we find, conditions here indicate sarcoma—that is a part of the karma of this body. These may be aided, but as to correcting entirely—the suggested applications will only be helpful for the conditions.

[Plantain and ultra-violet light were recommended as treatment.]

These will bring ease. These will not cure, but are sources of help—and if studied—the juices of the plantain weed and the keeping away from certain food values— help may be brought even to many individuals suffering with same.

Do these for the helpful forces of this body. Do those things suggested that will help if applied consistently.

(3387-1)

Probably the most interesting case of physical karma in the Edgar Cayce files is that of a young girl of seventeen, who was suffering from a painful hip condition—incipient cancer of the bone. Certainly we have more intimate details on this case for she was told of a specific act which was the origin of the karma or problem.

During the period of Nero's reign in Rome, in the latter portion of same, the entity was then in the household of Parthesias—and one in whose company many became followers of, adherents to, those called Christians in the period, and during those persecutions in the arena when there were physical combats. The entity was a spectator of such combats, and under the influence of those who made light of them; though the entity felt in self that there was more to that held by such individuals, as exhibited in the arena, but the entity—to carry that that was held as necessary with the companionship of those about same—laughed at the injury received by one of the girls [301] in the arena, and *suffered* in *mental anguish* when she later on became cognizant of the physical suffering brought to the body *of* that individual during the rest of the sojourn. The suffering that was brought was of a *mental* nature, and when music—especially of the lyre, harp, or of the zither—was played, the entity *suffered* most; for the song and the music that was played during that experience brought—as it were—the experience to the entity. Hence in meeting same in the present, there has been builded that which the entity passes through, or 'under the rod'— as it were—of that as of being pitied, laughed at, scorned, for the inability of the personal body to partake of those in the material activities as require the need of all the physical body; yet in the music, in the acceptance, in the building of those forces through that which laughed at, which scorned—though knowing; now *knowing*, laugh to scorn those who would *doubt* the activities of the forces that build in a material body that activity in every cell, every force, to make a perfect body.   (275-19)

48.

Though Partheniasi (her Roman name) later suffered remorse and mental anguish because of her act and the Christian girl's agony, in this life her own hip bone was being gnawed by a disease diagnosed as incurable. The doctors had even suggested amputation. She was paying in the same coin she had meted out.

This case had many interesting aspects. For although this was a case described as incipient cancer (technically identified as osteochondritis, or Perthes' Disease), and pronounced incurable, the patient did gradually recover by adhering to the regimen outlined in the readings. The young lady, in fact, had a total of forty-five readings, most of them pertaining to her physical condition and treatment. A few were life readings, however, giving details of her earlier development and former family relationships.

In this girl's first physical reading, the question was asked if her condition could be brought to normal and a "perfect cure." The answer: "Depends entirely upon the response of the body, the awakening of that within the forces of the body itself, of the accumulated forces, as may be brought by the mental forces, applied with those of the material. (275-1)"

In other words, the cure would depend as much on the girl's mental attitude as on the physical applications.

A reading given a little later offered real hope and is in sharp contrast to the less promising prognosis already noted in some of the cancer cases previously reported here. While stating that the response to treatment would not be "quick," the reading pointed out that once begun *properly*, the recovery process would be "sure and certain."

The girl came to realize that she was meeting herself, and asked:

How can I make good karma from this period?
As has been given as to what karmic influence is, and what one must do about same. Lose self in the consciousness of the *indwelling* of the Creative Force, in that

channel as has been prepared for the escape of the sons *and* daughters of men, through the *Son* of man! This is the escape, and what to be done about it! Lose self; make His will one with *thy* will, or thy will be lost in *His* will, being a *channel* through which He may manifest in the associations of self with the sons and daughters of men!   (275-23)

Some other interesting questions arose in later readings, such as:

Why did the entity wait until this incarnation to make good karma from the Roman period?
Because it couldn't do it before!
How many other lives have I had in between the one you have mentioned through this source?
(After long pause). In earth's sphere, two. (Pause) *Life has continued!*   (275-25)

When she asked who the martyred Christian girl of the Roman times was today, the girl was told it was one near and dear to her! In fact, it was her brother's wife, who also acted as her nurse, and was serving her in Christian love and kindness.

One of the suggestions given to this girl was to study the harp. In a much earlier life, in Egypt, she had been one of the first to use the harp or lyre. This music, it was explained, would help her to meet the things she had to overcome, and would be an outlet for her higher nature; for she had developed spiritually and gained much in the life in Egypt.

Some of the spiritual counsel which helped her was in reading 275-19:

Give exact guidance how entity can best make good her karma during this life.
As has been outlined, that—now knowing that as is to be met, no scorn, no sneers, but with patience, with fortitude, with praise, with the giving of pleasure in music, in

kindnesses, in gentle words, in bespeaking of that as may build for a perfect mind, a perfect soul, a perfect body, [by these] may the entity overcome those things that have beset—that not often understood, those things that so easily beset us; making the will one with the Creator and the Creative Forces. Be used by *them*, and the channel—the cup—will run over with blessings. Those things that easily beset bespeak not of those only that are weaknesses in the flesh; but the weaknesses in the *flesh* are the scars of the soul, and these, only in that of making the will one with His, being washed—as it were—in the blood of the lamb. (275-19)

"*Scars of the soul*"! Can one imagine a more vivid or accurate phrase to put into proper perspective our fleshly ills? It certainly tells us what physical karma is all about.

This girl had been told in other readings that she had two earth lives between the Roman one and her present life. She asked about a particular relationship in the present that had its roots in the Roman incarnation, and was given an interesting reply:

What ideals from that time [Roman] prompted us to come together now in this present relationship?
The ideals as set by those in their union, and each soul finding the channel, the opportunity for the expression in this experience for that needed in its own soul development as related to each of the others in this experience.

Not only that as has been called karma, for these—as seen by that given—have to deal with and to do with what individuals have done with their knowledge of their opportunities in experiences *to* the Creative Forces as manifested by the environ in that experience. It's well for you to analyze that! (275-38)

And yet in another reading, this further advice was given:

It may be well for the entity to know that each soul, each entity, each activity, must be of the development within self that there may be, through the actions in thought, in deed, in fact, those things that make for the continuity of that which may be spoken or acted in the associations with others. So does the impelling influence come into the experience of each soul in its journey through an experience.   (275-35)

The girl seemed to meet the spiritual requirements to overcome her karma, for her hip finally healed and she lived a useful, constructive life as a teacher for many years. Today, however, she is recovering from an accident to her back—an injury that has had complications relating to the original weakness in the hip. One must ponder the apparent implications of the renewal of her suffering.

Stroke

The Edgar Cayce Foundation lists stroke cases under apoplexy as a medical classification. Dr. William A. McGarey, Director of the A.R.E. Clinic, Phoenix, Arizona, explains this and describes apoplexy as follows in a circulating file on the subject:

Apoplexy—or apoplectic stroke—is medically known to be a sudden collapse with partial or complete paralysis on one side, usually associated with high blood pressure. In the benign form, there is a spasm or a minor hemorrhage in the brain tissue. In the malignant form, on the other hand, there is sudden massive hemorrhage in the brain tissue causing a sudden loss of consciousness and coma.

It appears that strokes are a physical condition we bring upon ourselves by our dietary habits and daily living. Stress is ever more present today in our lives, and this does have an effect on the circulation; so in most cases of stroke, we may be dealing with "cash" karma more than a deep-seated problem from a past life.

Dr. McGarey further explains the condition of apoplexy in these words:

Apoplexy is a disease process involving primarily the circulatory system as a whole, but including the make-up of the cells and substances within the blood, the flow, the circulation, the pressures within the circulation and the integrity of the vessel walls. Apparently the control of the circulatory system as a whole lies within the sympathetic nervous system throughout its entire length from the coccygeal nerves up to the medulla oblongata. And this control includes not only the balancing or the coordinating between the deep and the superficial circulation, but extends even to the maintenance or control of the platelets or the tendency to form clots; the production of the other formed elements (the white and red cells) within the circulatory system; and the production of those substances which control the integrity of the walls of the veins and the arteries.

The Wall Street Journal for July 18, 1979, reports that this disease strikes over 400,000 Americans every year; that it kills half of them and leaves the rest disabled for months or even years. Thus, it does take a big toll in medical expenses and careers.

One stroke victim had three readings from Edgar Cayce, the first being a life reading. This gives us some insight into his personality and problems. It does indicate, I think, that he was working on karmic emotional problems. The excerpt given here offers some general information on karma that would apply to *anyone*.

As in all of the life readings given by Cayce, astrological information is also given. Apparently this fellow gave in to the temptations of Martian tendencies in one lifetime and allowed anger to build up excessively. In the present lifetime, the entity is meeting self, or what he has built through his own consciousness; for the readings repeatedly stress the fact that mind is ever the builder. The anger and strife have resulted in a karmic residue, finding expression in impaired circulation and, eventually, a stroke. Yet at any time, through the application of free will which is the gift of the Creator to man, he could have reversed these negative influences and their ill effects by developing in his character such opposite and positive qualities as tolerant compassion and patience, thus erasing his karma, or the natural consequences of the law of cause and effect, as it might be termed. That seems to be the thrust of the following trance-state comments by Cayce:

Know that while astrological and earthly sojourns *are* as omens or signs, or inclinations, the influences of will as respecting the knowledge and the application of Creative Forces in the experience of an entity far surpass or exceed an astrological or even a material sojourn.

For each soul enters an earthly experience with problems within its own experience, as well as for relationships that are to be met in the light of constructive influences.

For while there is prepared in the experience of each individual the ways and means through which the soul may attain its understanding, and there is the advocate with the Father through the Son, each soul—as the Son manifested in the flesh—meets those experiences.

For if ye would be like Him, put on Him, that He may stand with thee in those periods when doubt or fear arises, or when those influences arise from the very association of spirit with matter—that becomes the experience of each soul.

For it is the soul that seeks its companionship with its Maker, and in the flesh finds means of expressions that make forever true that as He has given, 'As ye do it unto these, the least of these my children, ye do it unto me.'

So in the experience of each soul, not only are they to become opportunities for self-expression but that others, too—through the experiences of their association—may bring into their own experience their relationships as one to another.

In the Martian influence, there are those tendencies for anger, strife, relationships of this character between nations or groups or individuals to at times become as a portion of the entity's experience—whether as personal or as the entity's experience, making for those influences in which the entity may oft be misjudged as to his purposes or as to his acclaims and his activities.

The more efficient an individual finds itself, the more obligations, the more responsibilities are required. In this is the saying true that 'whom the Lord loveth He chasteneth, and purgeth every one.' For of him to whom much is given is much expected.

Though the natural inclinations come for rule by self, yet these tempered with those influences and forces for patience and mercy and justice would be helpful. (1211-1)

This reading indicates that this man had been a teacher during the time the Master walked on the earth, and his prior life was a great influence in the present. A question he asked indicates family problems which obviously begin in a previous life:

Please state the relation in previous experiences with the members of my immediate family.

Where the activities of the family were in associations, when comparisons are drawn from the activities of each, it may be seen how the friendships and the relationships in each made for what may be termed the *necessity* of their *closer* relationships in the present. These sought by self in that as has been given, makes them become of a deeper meaning. (1211-1)

His second reading, on his physical health, indicates a need for a change in attitude:

It becomes much of a mental and a spiritual attitude of the body. True, physical is physical, mental is mental, and spiritual is spiritual. Yet these are one in their manifestations in the material forces of the body. And so long as resentment is held, so long as disturbing conditions exist and there is not compliance with all the laws of each in their various phases of applications for the body, incoordination and disturbing factors arise. (1211-2)

The karmic imputations are fairly evident. A later physical reading deals more with the physical aspects of the case:

As we find, there has come about that which we have indicated was to be prevented—from the lack of consistency in keeping the coordination between the superficial and deeper circulation, both as to nerve impulse and blood supply as well.

Thus, the arterial circulation has been so overfilled as to cause seepages through the thinned walls.

We would have, consistently, for periods of two to three weeks, the hydrotherapy treatments. (1211-3)

Paralysis

Paralysis is sometimes confused with apoplexy. For example, in reading 3056-1, the sufferer was told, "This is not a stroke, it is paralysis." General paralysis does appear to be similar to apoplexy, or at least the resulting physical symptoms are nearly identical. The physical cause, however, is different. Apoplexy deals more with the circulation, while paralysis is more of a nerve condition. Another victim of paralysis asked:

Any other suggestions for this body at this time, or for those who are treating the body?

Remember that given, there is a privilege, there is a duty, in each. Many might ask, or self might ask, why such conditions came into the experience of either those that must minister or those that must wait. That ye may know the better the acceptable year, the acceptable day, of the Lord. (448-2)

This next case, involving facial paralysis, was clearly of karmic origin. No doubt details of this entity's prior lives would be interesting and instructive, showing the effect of emotions on the physical:

Why did I have to go through this life with facial paralysis?
Because thou didst lose in the beauties of thy own experience, in the beauties as the queen, in the beauties as the princess—or as she to whom much conscience was given, that ye besmeared in the first and that ye feared in the second. They only find expressions that in the present become rather those things in patience, in tolerance, in hope, in long-suffering—that ye may know indeed the true light. (1298-1)

Case 448—already quoted in part—is included because of the counsel given on attitude and healing. Also, it emphasizes the importance of adhering to the recommended treatment. Apparently this person had not made the necessary effort and had been quite remiss in connection with following the given instructions and in using the recommended battery device mentioned in his reading, called a "Radio-active Appliance." (This device, although not "radio-active" in a literal sense, involves a redistribution of the body's own electrical currents. It is mentioned in a number of the Edgar Cayce readings as an aid to healing.)

Yes, we have the body here; this we have had before.

Not so much change in the general physical forces of the body and their reactions from that we have last had here.

While there are some improvements in the *physical* forces of the body, the mental and its reaction upon the applications made for corrections—producing disappointing activities in the body—has its effect. Yet, as we find, there has not been the adherence to those things that were outlined for the body, in a consistent and persistent manner, save for *only* a short time.

And, as the very nature of the disturbance has been for the tendency of an atrophied condition in ganglia and centers, and there has not been the stimulation sufficient for the creating of the impulses to revive or revivify those portions, the improvement has not been in the directions as was even suggested.

Let's for the moment analyze conditions-physical, conditions-mental, and that necessary for improvements in such an application.

Whenever there was given the spiritual healing, either from Elijah, Elisha, Samuel or the Master, did the individuals obtain it by conforming to the suggestions half-heartedly and in part?

Would a dipping in Jordan six times have healed Naaman? [II Kings 5:14]

Would the breathing once into the body of the widow of Zarephath's son have brought life? [I Kings 17:21]

Did the clay and the washing of same in Siloam heal, or was it all a story? [Luke 17:14]

What is the law in material things?

Ye are subject to those laws under which the conditions have been brought about in thine body, in thine mind! The *spirit* IS willing, the flesh *is* weak.

That an impingement brought the lack of impulse to the body is a fact. And the application of only a portion of the treatment suggested is the same as dipping once or twice.

Either apply that given, or make thine self as one that,

'I know, but I won't do it.'

In making the application in the present, then, let's turn for the present to this:

See that the applications of the Radio-active Appliance are in order, all connections in line. It *is* necessary that there be the cold from ice in order to make the correct applications, but these may be given correctly.

And go to Dobbins—without cost, without price—and let him *make* the adjustments, and the applications of the rubs as given, that the vibrations to create a balance in the circulation may be effective.

Do that.

It is *worth* MAKING the try. Or forget it altogether.

(448-3)

Accidents

Accidents have been increasing as cars and traffic increase. One would not, at first, expect an accident to be physical karma; for an accident seems to be a matter of chance, and wholly in the present. Yet, a seeming "accident" is often the incident which triggers a karmic condition that was awaiting its time, as it were. Diabetes, for example, frequently seems to appear as the result of an accident. The shock presumably causes a glandular disturbance.

The readings, on occasion, gave warnings about accidents, and in other instances reported the condition resulting from an accident to be karmic. The parents of one girl were warned to be careful of their daughter so as to avoid an accident. Her reading indicated that she was accident-prone as a result of an accident which caused her death in her last earth-life.

Before this the entity was in the household of the Audubons. There the entity was the daughter of the present mother, and not too long-lived in that experience. For, the entity then was destroyed—or met sudden death—in an accident, in a car, or a horse and car.

59.

These are latent conditions in the present experience for the entity, then; and warnings must be entertained and kept, not as to keeping the entity from such, but *know* with whom any traveling is done—else there may be accidents in car or in travel that may make of the body a partial invalid. These are a part of the karma, unless there is kept that law of grace through which karma is *not* an actual experience.

Hence there shall be great stress in the unfoldment of development of the entity, upon its trust in DIVINE sources, of its care, of its intent, of its *trust* in those with whom it becomes active—not as to *daring*, but as for purpose, as for hope, as for those forces of the divine nature; that the entity in its intent and purposes may be kept in a sound, perfect body to better fulfill its purpose in the earth in its present sojourn.   (1635-3)

A particularly dramatic case of physical karma triggered by an accident involved a 24-year-old man who was paralyzed from the neck down as the result of an automobile wreck. In 1926, following three unsuccessful operations, his case was brought to Cayce's attention and a reading was requested. But since the request was for a *physical* reading, the revelation of a prior-life experience—contained at the very end of the reading, and given in a scarcely audible aside by the sleeping Cayce—was not included in the written report of the reading mailed off to the young man in question. It might have proved to be more than he could bear, in his present stage of development.

Now, the experience of this entity through this present physical plane, as a developing entity through earth's experiences, would be more interesting than the physical conditions, for these are of the nature that, while assistance and relief may be brought, there is little to be done to bring the normal forces of the body, save through untiring energy, trouble, patience, and persistence, for in the cervical and the first dorsal we find there was in times back that condition existing in which a portion of the cartilaginous forces between the vertebrae was crushed. Not sufficient to injure the spinal cord direct, save as to cause that to bring about such conditions as to ward off, or prevent, the flow of energy.

Keep the whole mentality in that way as to build the best development, for, as has been seen, many of these conditions are merited through those actions of the mental forces of the body. Hence that as given in the first. *[Then, in a scarcely audible aside]:* See, this is Nero.   (33-1)

Poorly educated in the present, and dependent upon Christian charity for the remainder of his relatively short life (he reportedly died some eighteen years later, without any visible improvement in his condition), an incident subsequent to the reading suggests that this man was perhaps not mentally or spiritually ready, this time around, to cope with the truth about his karma face to face. For in 1928, two years after his reading, he wrote (or dictated) a letter to Mr. Cayce containing a bold proposition, much in the imperious manner, one might suspect, of the Emperor Nero himself! His words: "I rec'd a letter telling me you have your hospital fixed ready...if you say you can cure me, I will give you $1,000, and if you don't you won't get anything. Isn't that fair?"

Needless to add, his offer was not accepted.

Diabetes

Diabetes, a disorder of sugar metabolism in which the individual produces inadequate insulin, is partly genetic and strongly influenced by diet, weight, and stress. It provides us with two karmic cases in the readings. One of them, reading 953-7, gives an incident in a previous life which would make one think a balancing process was in operation. The person involved was told that his current problem stemmed from a lifetime in early America when he was a stool-dipper. Possibly he enjoyed his job a little too much, for his reading indicates the underlying emotional problem as self-aggrandizement!

This same reading is also interesting because it is one of the early ones in Mr. Cayce's long career. It took place on December 23, 1923, in Dayton, Ohio. The suggestion given was for a "horoscope reading." The client had fifteen readings in all, so he did show an interest in details and was continually searching for inner causes. Happily, he was told that he had overcome the destructive forces from his earlier life in America, and evidently he made good development in this life. The reading in particular reference here is brief, so it is presented in its entirety:

You will give detailed information relative to the appearance of the soul and spirit of that body in the Puritan forces as given in horoscope reading of November 9th.

In this we find the appearances were in those that brought destructive forces through the self-aggrandizement through the will as brought in that of the ruling elements to those that were given to bring the thoughts of the spirit forces of others to the plains people. Yes, he acted here in the form of stool-dipper.

What are the characteristics exhibited in the present entity from that appearance?

The study of those forces, and in the questioning of self and individual self as to those characters as brought the destructive forces to self through that period, or place, or sphere. This is opposite to those at present, as we have outlined.

Follow those. Keep close to the right and narrow way, giving understanding that development from each and every entity must be upon its own force, with love and charity to all, and giving the best of self to build that which is the real in every plane, the spirit force, or the companion to the soul of every entity.   (953-7)

A later reading reported improvement and promised a cure if directions were followed.

Now the conditions are very good, compared to those we have had from time to time. The strain on the system through mental and physical have and show their reflection in the system from time to time. The condition, though, that produces the diabetic effect in the body is being gradually relieved. The action of the system against the creating of those conditions as have produced this effect in the body are of the nature that received impressions through mental and physical conditions both. This, then, as we find, only needs the care and attention, the persistence as will bring the better conditions for this body, keeping the medicinal properties as have been given.

Will this diabetic condition be entirely cured if these instructions are followed?

Be entirely removed from the body, or to such an extent there will be no return, save under the strain of the weakened condition produced in the organs that are involved in the condition. That is, though [from] the body may be entirely removed, too much sugars, too much stimulants, too much of *any* condition producing strain would bring a return, as we have had in some forms in body during the past. As we find at the present, there are some conditions in the body where there is a show of eliminations not being set just properly, from conditions in the circulation. This we find temporary and produced by a contraction through conditions created in digestion.

(953-14)

The next reading, for a different sufferer of diabetes, emphasizes the need for an attitudinal change. Oneness of body, mind and spirit—creating balance and harmony—was an aspect of self-realization essential to the entity's recovery.

Hence there is easily seen—and it becomes a significant fact—that the basis or the cause, or that producing the disturbance, has not been reached; and while the body, the mental abilities of the body, above the ordinary, and while the body within itself is pyschic in the manner wherein that the applications of laws, truths and tenets as may be set forth by the body *mind* of the body would apply, and do apply *well*, in the lives of others; yet apparently the body within itself has not been able, and is *not* able, to create that sufficient attitude to meet the needs for the physical conditions of the body. This great lesson the body then should take to self, for self, and in giving same to others in the tenets, in the lessons, in the truths as being set forth; that is, that the body—physically, mentally, spiritually—is one *body*; yet, in the varied conditions as arise within a physical body, these must often be treated as a unity—that is, each element treated as a unit—yet in the fullest application they are *one*. Hence, as has been given concerning physical conditions in others, here we find physical must be *met* with physical and the *alone* application of mental and physical are not sufficient any more than the purely spiritual and *mental* is sufficient for purely physical conditions, that must be met with the elements and laws as control physical effects created in a physical living organism! While a physical living organism represents to the sensuous mind of man that of the full complete elements of every element contained within the universe—for it is a portion, or a universe within itself—yet when one element has become so out of balance with another in a physical organism that destructive forces are created within the elements of the vibratory forces as are set in motion within the body, or each unit of the body within itself is as a full cellular organism and a portion of the whole of the universal whole, and when one of these—or many of these—as in the instance of this organism of the body—becomes so unbalanced as to need the correction within self, then we find that the body is to be applied in physical manner toward that which will in the *physical* sense meet the needs of that unbalanced, or that uncoordinating element *within* the physical, as to make it one again *with* the whole element and thus bring the better or nearer normal conditions for a body; for, as is seen within this physical organism, all of the life—all of the lives—all of the karmic influences have to do with conditions existent in the physical body. Hence when one vibratory force within an element becomes out of attunement with the whole, there may be expected that attribute responding within that physical organism that will prevent the full attunement of the body to the whole. Hence the necessity of *meeting* the conditions in the proper way and manner.

When the digestive system, then, became so out of balance through karmic influences—or through that as may be termed pre-dispositioned of conditions in the body— and the physical action of the body was such as to keep these in attunement with same, rather than correcting same within the physical forces—then we brought about these disturbing elements. Though no organic heart trouble exists, organic trouble with the pancreas and the liver and kidneys *does* exist.

These are, then, uncorrected vibratory forces as are set within the body of this *entity*, or the body here known as the body given. These bring forces, then, uncomplimentary to the mental and physical being of the body, creating fear, creating elements within self as prevent the proper attributes. Yet there is often seen, even under the stress and strain, the body brings—through the mental, and through the brain and spiritual forces of the body—that which is *wonderful* to be understood by others, and even that that others *applying* in their *own* lives may be awakened to the spiritual forces as are manifest through the many psychic forces of a living human body in the material sensuous plane; yet in the very act that the body

65.

is not able to attune self in the same force, under the same environmental conditions under which the body finds many of those whom the body would aid, assist and direct—this in itself brings to the body those things that are detrimental in the development of the mental, spiritual and soul body of this entity in itself. Then, necessarily, we meet the needs of the physical forces as applied in the body.

In the mental forces of the body—work out thine own salvation in fear and trembling, giving thine self to the powers that be, that self may be used as an instrument of service to others in directing them in the writings that the body may give.   (2263-1)

Tuberculosis

At one time, tuberculosis was also classified as a "big killer." Today it is reportedly on the increase again, perhaps because of its prevalence among Southeast Asian refugee groups and other poverty-level immigrants, although in 1950 the scourge of tuberculosis had almost been wiped out in America. Many of the large sanitariums for treatment of tubercular patients, such as the one at Lake Placid, New York, were closed down years ago because they were no longer needed. (Thus we can observe the cyclical behavior of certain disease patterns in human society.)

Tuberculosis is caused by a germ, the tubercle bacillus; it is more likely in individuals in poor general health. Alcoholics, smokers, and those with poor hygiene are the most susceptible, but anyone can contract this infection. If the victim is in good health, however, he can handle the infection well and develop a relative immunity to it.

In reading 3671-1, we find an interesting karmic case of tuberculosis, for its origins were traced to an apparent "accident" in infancy, and demonstrates that karma applies to infectious diseases as well as other types.

The background report on this case was given orally just

prior to the reading. The report stated that this individual dis-
located his hip when he was only two years old. This was an
accident which occurred when he tried to crawl out of his crib,
catching his leg and pulling the hip out of place. This resulted
in his spending many of his early years in plaster casts. The
doctor finally gave him up as a bad job, expecting him to die.
He clung to life, however, and at age 22 asked for a physical
reading from Edgar Cayce. It should be mentioned, perhaps,
that this young man had spent a considerable part of his early
years in the Children's Seashore Hospital, in Atlantic City, tied
down to a board, strapped across the chest, with casts on both
legs. The hip bone being out of place caused a new socket to
form, which in time caused rubbing against the pelvis. By age
22, the young man's disease was diagnosed as tuberculosis of
the bone. It was a pitiable case.

As we find, there are disturbing conditions that prevent
the better physical functioning of this body. While in a
general manner, or in material expression, all of this arises
from the lack of judgment or lack of consideration—as
accidents—we find that, if the body will accept and act
upon it, it is meeting its own self in a measure from karmic
conditions.

Thus there may be material aid, there may be mental and
spiritual aid in such ways as to bring better conditions, as
well as soul and spiritual development.

To be sure, there are physical or pathological conditions
existent—yet the beginning should be in self.

Do not blame others, do not condemn anyone for the disturbances that exist. Know that there are healings for the
body, else the opportunities would not have been given the
body in the resuscitation. Know deep within self that God
hath need of thee at this time. Know that He came into the
world that each individual, each entity, might have life
more abundantly; that is, more of life, more expectancy
from life, and more worthwhile experiences.   (3671-1)

Obviously this young man was in a lamentable condition. Yet his reading did give him hope, although he was told that he was meeting self. Unfortunately, we do not have a follow-up report as to whether his condition eventually improved, indicating some degree of success in meeting his karma.

Arthritis

Arthritis is a painful and crippling disease. Literally, arthritis is an "inflamation of the joints." There are many inter-related causes known to medical science: genetic patterns, immunological breakdowns, trauma, and chemical and nutritional deficiencies.

Based on the Cayce readings, arthritis is apparently a karmic condition, even though it does not appear at birth. The quotations from several readings given here point out the various immediate and inner causes of this condition. Something — diet, or whatever—triggers the problem, or causes it to manifest; but the inner, or root cause, has presumably been there right along, waiting to manifest when the physical organism is in a weakened or susceptible state. Externally viewed, the causal or motivative factor underlying an arthritic condition may be just the lack of good health habits, as here:

What is the cause of this condition?

It has been long coming on, or has existed for some time. The development of the condition is from the lack of the body's ability to eliminate properly. This is partly karmic, partly psychopathic, and partly of a purely pathological nature. (3015-1)

Or the immune system may be weak:

As we find, this condition arises from an infection that entered the body through those particular cycles of change when it became a part of the constitutional condition — or of the whole body; affecting it through the nerves, the bloodstream, the mental reflexes and reactions. Thus it becomes an insidious nature in the body. Thus it is partially a karmic condition.

To be sure, such an explanation would not be accepted by some. However, we will find that there must first be a change of attitude of the entity respecting spiritual things, finding the relationships within self with the Divine, and THEN making those very definite physical applications.

For all good and all healing must come from the Divine within each entity. And as the mental consciousness is made aware of the Divine within each individual cellular entity in the body-forces, there is the greater ability for the applications to contribute to the healing—by the use of that which attunes the body and body-functioning to the Creative Forces, or that shall answer to the destruction of that possessing the body in the way of those conditions causing the disturbance in the physical forces.

Do the first things first.

Do not begin to apply the material applications suggested, until the body comes to the physical and mental realization, through the study of divine manifestations in the earth, of the entity's relationship to that divinity; else the last estate will be worse than the first.   (3512-1)

Although proper diet and exercise are a necessity if good health is to be maintained, the inner cause, or dis-ease, may be emotional or attitudinal. All of these cases emphasize the need for spiritual attunement, as well as the need for correcting attitudes and emotions. Thus, the real or inner problem is on the mental or spiritual level. Since karma appears to be more of the spiritual than anything else, it would seem that the real work, the real effort, must be at the spiritual level if the condition is to be permanently corrected or healed.

Thus the beginning must be in the mental attitude of the body-mind. There must be kept a creative, constructive

69.

attitude, and not the condemning or faultfinding of others—which has been a portion of the karmic forces being met in self.   (3563-1)

That which is in the physical disturbing is, ever, the result of breaking a law; either pertaining to the physical, mental, or spiritual.   (3220-1)

Yes, as we find, while conditions are rather serious, there may be, with patience and persistence in the mental attitudes, as well as in the physical applications, help or relief, though not cure, for the body.

For these, as we find, are a part of the consciousness which has been builded, in the body-physical meeting itself in the mental and spiritual aspects of its use of life.

There are the conditions where the arthritic tendencies throughout all the segments of the spine, as well as in the structural portions in the extremities, are affected. Long ago, these might have been fully eradicated, but if there is in the present the radionic treatment in the radio short-wave length given the body, with the massages at least two to three times each week, these, we will find, will allow for more rest, less tensions in the body. The tendencies, throughout, to be tensions, will be lessened.   (3593-2)

While the direct cause of one woman's arthritis was a chemical imbalance, her attitude and basic selfishness were the real or inner causes of her problem:

What did I do to get this way?

The unbalancing in the chemical forces and the attitudes through some of the periods has much to do with the resultant physical conditions in the present. Hence the environs, the consistency and the purposefulness. Why would the entity be relieved of the disturbance? That it might gratify self alone, or that it might become a greater channel for activity as a witness-bearing entity for an ideal purpose? These are attitudes to consider.   (4040-1)

Cayce's secretary adds the note: "The song-and dance numbers which directly promoted her rise to fame were expressions of an attitude of selfishness and complete disregard for other people."
Excerpts from the following two cases provide us with additional insights on the relationship that appears to exist between karma and arthritis.

Now, while we find the conditions are apparently hopeless when it comes to a great deal of improvement—the deformities having been part of the karma, and the conditions that have arisen in the present experience, so that arms, limbs, all are deformed in a manner—there may be relief, though not curative measures.   (5068-1)

Is the condition physical in origin or mental?
It's more of the karmic nature. This, then, is mental and physical but let's begin with the first things first. As we go along we will change the attitude. For unless there is consistency and persistency, or unless something is to be done with the abilities of the body, with the abilities to be nearer normal in activity, why correct it at all?   (5120-1)

Asthma
Asthma is an illness in which recurrent spasms occur in the muscles of the bronchioles, resulting in gasping shortness of breath. It is thought to be partly genetic, environmental, psychological, and immunological in origin. Readings given for sufferers from this ailment seem to stress the need for personal work on the mental and spiritual level, and perhaps more markedly so than in the case of arthritic sufferers.

As we find, there are disturbances in the better physical

forces of the body. These are partially karmic, and thus there must be as much spiritual and mental application as physical. From the physical application indicated, there is also needed a great deal of spiritual awakening. (3359-1)

This next person, was told that he was meeting himself. And the reading makes it clear that he had been a hard task-master. In addition to an asthmatic condition, a lack of muscular control appeared to be involved as a critical aspect of his karmic indebtedness—for past deeds that were not revealed.

For here we have an individual entity meeting its own self—the conditions in regard to the movements of the body, the locomotories, the nerve ends, the muscular forces. What ye demand of others ye must pay yourself! Every soul should remember not to demand of others more than ye are willing to give, for ye will pay—and, as most, through the gills!

Then, when ye have found that these things are not helpful, we may give through these channels that which may be—if the body first begins to undertake to correct the attitude towards its fellow men, towards conditions and towards the world.

Make the world a better place in which to live. In whom and of what do you as a soul-entity obtain life and opportunity? What are you doing about it?

Consider and be wise. (3485-1)

The case which follows is somewhat similar, but was for a boy only twelve years old. He was told he had pressed the life out of others in a previous life; so now, as an asthmatic sufferer, he was experiencing the equivalency of having life pressed out of himself. Apparently the parents, too, were involved in the child's karma for "those responsible for the body" were admonished to provide the correct spiritual attitude within themselves, "set in that way of knowing the sources of forgiveness."

A cure was indicated for the boy if the proposed treatments were followed and the correct attitude maintained.

Here we have truly a pathological condition but a psychological as well as the physiological, and it extends to karmic reactions also. For one doesn't press the life out of others without at times seeming to have same pressed out of self.

If these disturbances are corrected pathologically in the early developing years, so that those pressures apparent in the areas from the 9th dorsal to the 1st cervical are corrected, we may allay oft those bronchial-asthmatic reactions that take the life and breath from the body.

The administration of other things outside are palliatives and will only bring about or create conditions that will not change.

Of course the hypodermics that may be given for such will relieve but will only produce stricture that would make for greater and greater disturbance as the body grows older.

It may be corrected osteopathically, it may require even six years—and a week's treatment out of each month during the whole six years, but it would be worth it for the body; provided the spiritual attitude of those responsible for the body, as well as the body, is set in that way of knowing the sources of forgiveness. For who can forgive sins save those against whom they are committed? And when one sins, the sin is against the giver of life, God.

(3906-1)

Reading 3661-1, given for a man of sixty, told him that he could achieve a change in his condition in spite of his age and the longstanding nature of the problem. This could be accomplished through changes in his mental and spiritual attitude. Scars in the upper dorsal and cervial area had affected the circulation.

These are partially karmic. While the age in the present and the longstanding conditions are against the body-physical, we find that the body mentally and spiritually can—through the spiritual and mental attitude of the body—change these to a great measure.

For who healeth all thy diseases? Who giveth life? Who is patient and kind? Who giveth every good and perfect gift?

Faith, hope and then the use of those measures that contribute physically to keeping this equal balance, and those mechanical changes that will correct the condition, will bring ease and help and eventually a complete cure—if these applications are carried forward coordinantly for the body.

Do the first things first. Make thy peace with thine own conscience and with thine own environ, and with those things that would hinder thee in any manner from being everything to thy neighbor, thy brother, thy friend, thy foe, that ye would have them to be to thee if conditions were reversed.   (3661-1)

Acne

Acne—a very distressing skin condition suffered by many teenagers—may be due to karma. Case 2709, a young girl of nineteen, was suffering both mentally and physically from this affliction. She had had this skin disorder since she was twelve or thirteen years old; and although she had tried various remedies, she had received no relief whatsoever. Actually the condition seemed to be getting worse. According to her reading, this condition was due to a previous life in France when she had incarnated as a man. She was told:

As we have indicated oft for others, we would again indicate for this entity; count it rather as an opportunity, a gift of a merciful Father, that there are the opportunities in the present for the sojourn in the material influences;

that the advantages may be taken of opportunities that come into the experiences, even though the hardships and disappointments have arisen.

Is there a karmic reason for my present skin disturbance—acne of the face?

Rather is it that of a glandular condition, as combined with a karmic condition from the experiences in the periods of the reconstruction in France.   (1709-3)

In a later reading she got some information on the role emotional disturbances may play:

Do emotional disturbances affect the skin on my face?

To be sure, emotional disturbances affect the *circulation;* causing the flushes which leave drosses, and naturally affect the superficial circulation.   (1709-5)

This imbalance was difficult to overcome but the young lady did receive help and her condition gradually improved.

Another case of acne was attributed to apparent overindulgence in a French period. Unfortunately we do not have a full report, but the difficulty, we are told, was definitely karmic:

Yes, we have the body and those conditions which are a part of the consciousness, aware and unaware, with the body-physical.

In giving the interpretation of the physical disturbances, many phases of this entity's experience should be taken into consideration. That there are physical disorders, and have been for some time, is self-evident. The sources of these are not so self-evident. For these are karmic conditions and the entity is only meeting its own self.

In the pathology or pathological conditions of the body, we find there has for some time been those disturbances with the activity of the glands of the eliminating system, so that there has come those physical disturbances in the

75.

form of acne and blemishes over various portions of the body; especially, face, arms, hands. (5092-1)

She was given some encouragement, however, in the concluding paragraph of her reading:

Let that mind be in thee as was in Him, who is the Way and the Truth and the Light, and we will make the light of love so shine through thy countenance that few, if any, will ever see the scars made by self-indulgence in other experiences. (5092-1)

Allergies
A woman suffering from allergies was told her condition was balancing the lingering effect of earlier experiences.

In another experience we find that the entity was a chemist, and she used many of those various things for the producing of itching in others. She finds it in herself in the present! And many of those things that produced the ability in the body for the breath itself to become poisonous to others in their associations. Just as the body finds in itself in the present, in the presence of certain metals, certain plastics, certain odors, the body immediately is poisoned. Just as certain characters of leathers. If these are tanned with oak, they do not harm the body. If they are tanned with those very same things the entity once used to hinder someone else, they hinder the entity. For, the cellular force in the mind has two points about each of the positive forces in mind with the cellular forces in the body, or red blood and white blood cells. For, about each is a positive and negative influence. These in the body have now become subject to such things.
What in leather reacts as a poison? Is it a single ingredient or a combination?
Depends upon what it has been tanned with as we have

indicated. If these are tanned in oak, they do not injure the body. The body is not allergic to those tanned in oak tanning. When tanned in those that are sympathic, or where there is the use of ash in same, these become poison to the body—the radiation from same. (3125-2)

For the conditions that are sought, then, have those products made from the ordinary woven cloth and not those things that are chemically produced. For as indicated, as the body used such in other experiences for destructive forces, it is meeting these in the present. But the change must be in self, not in trying to make everybody else change to suit your idiosyncrasies, as is understood. For physical effects are produced through the psychopathic conditions of the body forces. (3125-3)

Another allergy case is a bit vexing because it alludes to the karmic implications but gives no specifics. Yet it remains an intriguing case:

Now, we find there are abnormal conditions with this body. These are hidden in a manner, and are an interesting study from psychological and pathological conditions as come about in the variation of the effects as are produced by conditions that have not been easily understood, and dissension and discussion has often arisen as respecting that as produces same. *Most* interesting for this body would have been the experiences as produced same in the *entity's* experience. We deal with those in the present.

As is seen, the effect is almost diametrically opposed to what is ordinarily seen in effects upon a physical body; in that light, exposure, or any outside influence apparently produces a wreck to the whole system. This is a psychological condition, which is not easily understood, from even its name.

What will relieve the body now when exposed to the sun?

We must change the vibrations if we would have the *permanent* relief for the body. What will relieve at the present time? An overdose of gold! But that wouldn't be well for the body. Begin as we have outlined, if we would bring the better conditions for this body; for we must create in this body that of the engendered force to be able to overcome those incentives for the inner being, or the entity itself in past experiences. (5578-1)

Anemia

The following two excerpts from anemia cases give us further understanding of karmic conditions or causes.

As we find, there are disturbing forces. Some of these may be materially aided. Others must be met within self. If these conditions had been taken in times back, changes might have been wrought. In the present these are not necessarily karmic but if they are looked upon or accepted as such, then you will meet it. But these are physical and mental rather than the sources being spiritual directions misused. (3356-2)

The second case seems to be another example of karma's capacity to balance conditions from the past. In a former life, the person was responsible for much shedding of blood; now he finds himself the victim of anemia:

In the one before this we find in that land now known as Peru. The entity then one that rose in power over the Chum, and the entity overcame that ruler who lost self in the aggrandizement of selfish desires as respecting the fair sex; becoming the ruler, yet much *blood* was shed. Thence anemia. In this condition the entity gained physically, lost materially, gained mentally, lost in physical—in that the entity *learned* to know that service brought contentment, where power only brought dissension.

How may entity guard against this condition of anemia?

By applying that gained in knowledge as respecting the body, in self's own condition. That's given.   (4248-1)

Aphonia
(the inability to speak)

Here we have a case (which includes an interesting warning note on treatment by hypnosis) pointing out the apparent fact that a karmic condition is overcome or dissolved only by the application of one's own will. Despite external aids, which may be recommended and even prove helpful to a limited degree, no one can really meet a condition of this nature other than within self, where the causal factor lies.

Was this condition originally caused by a stroke or by emotional hysteria?

As indicated, emotional hysteria—as it arises from the *psychic* force of the body; producing a pathological condition, affecting those areas as indicated.

It is *not* mental.

Do these things, to be sure, as has been indicated.

The condition might be corrected almost instantly by the use of hypnosis, or by a series of some three or four such treatments; yet that overcoming that is necessary in the karmic influence of the body would *not* be met. Hence we would use the hypnosis method only as a last resort.

But, we find that it can be met in the manner here outlined, if there is that study, that prayer which will naturally arise by the meditations upon those portions of the promises of Creative Forces; for it will be met in Him.

For, all healing comes from the one source.   And whether there is the application of foods, exercise, medicine, or even the knife—it is to bring the consciousness of the forces within the body that aid in reproducing themselves—the awareness of creative or God forces.

(2696-1)

Congenital Abnormalities in Children

Children with congenital abnormalities represent perhaps the saddest and most pitiable example of physical karma. The readings for these children frequently said the condition was prenatal and that there was a lack of coordination in the physical between the cerebrospinal and other systems. Also, the statement was often made that the condition could be alleviated but not cured. Nor would the improvement happen overnight but would be a slow growth. Persistence and consistency were emphasized and required.

Moreover, it was frequently pointed out that this was karma for the parents as well as the child. Sometimes it seemed that the parents were even more involved than the child in the cause of the condition.

While the cases presented here are uniformly identified as karmic, the differences in the physical manifestation are interesting and revealing. The directions given the parents as to how they should work on the spiritual aspect of the case are also noteworthy.

Now, as we find, in considering those conditions as make for disturbances with this body, all phases of same should be considered. And unless there may be the full cooperative activities of all phases in bringing the experience to all alike, not a great deal of help or aid, as we find, may be expected.

True, there are definite pathological conditions. There are also psychopathic and metaphysical conditions.

While the individual entity or soul is in the experience meeting its own self, in doing this it is so bound up in the experiences of those that are responsible for the conditions that allow for the opportunity of expression in the individual, that these obligations, these needs for self-expression in these individuals are a part of that as may be necessary for the giving or the experiencing by the body of that as may bring a nominal, normal physical, mental and material expression for the body. This responsibility, because of its requirements of constant care and the necessary patience, the necessary long forebearance, cannot be delegated to others. For that *each* soul sows, so must it meet same.

That the conditions in the body of the entity, then, do not coordinate, is pathological; but that as is the cause primarily is rather metaphysical—in that the very natures arise from the bodies of those responsible for its entrance into the experience in those environs from these pathological views.

Then, if there is manifested or expressed the desire, the sympathy, the willingness for the activities of those who should care for the body, there may then be through such channels as these aids and helps given.

But that as is so close to the soul, to the very activity of same—how hath it been given about the pearls?

These should be then considered, these should be rather studied.

And when these have been agreed upon and indicated by those who are responsible in body, in mind, in self of same, we may aid.   (1314-1)

Here we have a clear case of the parents' responsibility. Indeed, "it cannot be delegated to others," they were warned! Moreover, this first reading indicates that no help could be given until the parents agreed to cooperate in every way. Since they requested a second reading, we can assume that they did accept their responsibility in connection with their little son's condition. The next reading indicates and reemphasizes the importance of the parents' cooperation and implies that there was a meaningful story to be told, if the past life of this entity were known. Did these parents sell or abandon their unwanted child in a past life? It is intimated. While treatments were recommended for this child, the emphasis was on the need of the parents to pray and meditate while giving the treatments.

Yes, as we find, as has been indicated, the conditions while represented in pathological reactions arise from that which is at times called a karmic condition.

Hence they become psychological and metaphysical as well. Thus in bringing any permanent relief for the inco-ordinations that exist in the physical forces of this body, must include activities of those that are responsible for the physical manifestation of the body, the mind, the soul in the present.

That in the formations through the physical functioning there are adherences in the tissue in the body that prevents the nominal or normal reaction through the sensory reactions of the body is apparent.

That these conditions arise from associations and activities of all associated in same is not apparent, yet must be taken into consideration in activities for helpful applications; else we will find the last estate—in the *physical* reaction in the present—worse than the first.

Much might be given as respecting this association, and a pattern of same may be seen in the selling of Joseph into Egypt; used for a saving of those to whom the promise was given. And the same here may be applicable if there will be the whole of the influence applied in the manner as may be and as is indicated from the pathological, the psychological and the metaphysical conditions in the minds, the purposes, the desires of all.

In the physical forces (pathologically) we find the lacteals, as related to the assimilation and the activities in the body of the glandular forces as create the blood supply, as create the elemental factors in the activity of the system, inactive in some, overactive in others.

During the whole periods, each evening—as the application of the Radio-active Appliance are made, during the 30-minute period of this application to the extremities of the body—let the parents, in meditation over and with the body as it begins its slumber, give these, not merely as words but in their *own* words, but these as the essence, as the purposes, as the saying:

"The Father of light and mercy and truth, create in this body that as will bring the perfect coordination of the members of the body itself, that the soul may manifest in a perfect body.

"These we seek through the faith in thy promises to those who call on thee, that thou wilt hear and answer speedily.

"Thanking thee for thy mercy, for thy care, for thy love, this we offer in humbleness of thy name, O God!"

These continued daily, these brought into the daily application with others, with thy care, with thy love, will bring help, hope and understanding to all.

These words of the prayer keep earnestly day by day, at the same periods that there is the application of those vibratory forces in the body, as are set in motion by the reaction of those influences created in the Radio-active Appliance—which will bring, does bring, *unison* to the body, to the mental forces, to the nerve energies of all.

We are through for the present.   (1314-2)

There is no report on this case as to whether the applications were given or how effective they were.

Another case, diagnosed as mongoloidism, gives further insight into the karma of abnormal children. Mongoloidism is a congenital abnormality of the brain which leads to severe mental retardation. It is often associated with massive heart defects.

A letter from the father of this child, requesting a reading for his mongoloid daughter, explained the background:

[When] she was born...in delivery we noticed a depression on each side of her skull at temporal area; for several weeks she made no sound and found difficulty in nursing; unable to walk until 3½ years of age; did not talk until

6 years and unable to make distinct words or carry on natural conversation as there is no continuity of thought or definite coordination of mental processes; seems to understand what is told to her but unable to make her own thoughts register; concentration is almost nil although she can listen to the radio and pick out the tunes on the piano; she loves music and pictures; can take care of her personal needs but we have someone to watch over her all the time; is short of stature and somewhat heavy.

Medical doctors at first said she was a mongolian type and would not live to be 6 years old but that thyroid tablets might help and these were given for quite a while, then manipulative treatment was used and she improved very definitely up to a certain point and has remained thus ever since. Can anything further be done for her?

At the time of the reading, the girl was already 20 years of age and obviously a great care for the parents. Said the reading:

Yes, yes, here we have an entity meeting its own self. These are not desirous and yet it is for the unfoldment and development of this soul-entity. Physically, only helpful influences may be brought for the mental and soul-self. Much may be the contribution for this entity in the present in kindness, patience, love. All of these are needed in the body. These will aid the soul. For, remember, *the soul never forgets*, and that which is practiced to the soul, in the soul, will bring eventually a growth in knowledge, in the understanding of the love of the Creative Forces.

Hence we find an individual entity born not only to be a charge to the parents but it is needed for the parents as well as needed by the entity. (5335-1)

The parents were advised to use the Wet Cell Appliance (another electrical device, which was described in the Edgar Cayce readings and, like the Radio-active Appliance, recommended in special cases). Chloride of gold sodium was a part of the appliance treatment, to be followed with massage.

> Do this regularly and will not only find help to the body (not curative but a help to the body) but a more gentle and a better activity throughout the body.
> Don't put the body away, it needs the love, the attention.
>
> (5335-1)

Could there be a more poignant bit of advice for the parents of any abnormal child than is contained in that last line?

In 1949, several years after Edgar Cayce's death, his secretary Gladys Davis wrote to the girl's father as a routine procedure in updating the physical readings wherever treatment had been recommended but no follow-up report received. The father's response, in a letter dated April 26, 1949, was brief:

> Treatment suggested in the reading was followed for three months; [she] showed no change at time nor any since. We pinned our last hope on the reading...be glad to hear from you at any time; we greatly appreciate kind thoughts expressed in your letter.

Should the treatment have been continued longer? Perhaps something could have been accomplished with persistence and patience.

The mother of another mongoloid child had a reading in which she asked questions relating to the abnormality and the reason for the child's condition. There is a suggestion that some of the reason could be traced to a former life of the mother's, when the Master walked the earth. Yet the woman was told not to blame herself, or anyone else, but to accept her sorrow and give the child the needed, loving care. Thus she would be able to make her atonement.

Prior to the reading the mother submitted the following questions to be asked of the sleeping Cayce, in trance state:

Are there any conditions in past lives of either myself or husband that have a bearing or relationship on the abnormality of our daughter...6 years old, which condition has been diagnosed as mongolian idiocy from infancy?

How may I best help her?

Is it possible for me to have normal children?

What have been my past relationships with my husband?

What is the lesson I am to learn from my child's affliction?

Somewhat later, a letter was received from the husband, pointing out that his wife was in labor pains, and momentarily expecting the birth of another child. They were anxious to know the prognosis for the mental health of the expected baby, apparently fearing another mongoloid child. A reading was given a few days later.

Yes, we have the records here. Not all are pretty, yet we have many talents, many abilities which are latent and manifested in the experience of this entity through the earth's sojourn, as well as in those interims between the manifestations of the entity, or of the soul, as an individual entity in the material plane.

We would choose from these records that which if applied in the present experience may bring a greater harmony, a greater purposefulness into the experience of the entity through this particular sojourn.

The experience in the earth in the present has in many ways so far been disappointing. The abilities of the entity to create words which would be pictures of the emotions of the body, these have been denied the body, yet in the entity's own environ, yea, in its own home, are those sorrows, which used as a basis, may bring forth that which may be most helpful, not only in creating a better understanding and purpose in the life experience of the entity, but the remuneration for same (which the entity cares little for as of itself) may be part of the experience.

Thus the entity has a passionate nature, fondness for affection, and this in particular has been denied, and the entity often is lonely deep within self.

Know that this earth is not thy own, and the purpose in the earth is to prepare the soul-body for companionship with its Maker, God.

Thus seek, don't blame creative energies, don't mourn for that which cannot be helped, but do find within self that desire for that which ye may do or say towards individuals, for others.

Show forth the love ye know, ye may appreciate, which the Father showeth to the children of men in the gift of His son, thy brother, that ye might have eternal life.

Then as to the sorrow, which is to be a portion of thy present experience, accept it, not reject it, nor attempt to put it away. Be gentle, be kind, be patient, be long-suffering, and it will bring greater joy, greater harmony within thy experience and you may be very sure that the next child which comes to thee with that ideal will not only be beautiful in body and in mind but may be a real blessing to many, especially in the study of what causes the activities in relationships with individuals producing such as thy present sorrow.

Either, then, as the study of the spiritual life or that which may be presented in the anatomical structure of body, mind and soul, may that soul which will be thy next companion in childbirth bring to the world helpful forces, that less and less of such may be the lot of man, if parents will but listen.

Do not blame self; do not blame thy companion, do not blame God. For it is self and thy companion meeting thyselves in those conditions that this soul, too, may one day walk closer to God. For He, thy Father God, hath not willed that any soul should perish but hath with every temptation prepared a way for forgiveness, and thus may this soul in thy child now that hath caused so much, does cause so much sorrow, yet, through thy closer walk with thy God, know, too, the joy of the Fatherhood of God, the brotherhood of man, the redeeming love of Jesus Christ.

These should be the attitudes and let not any influence take that hope, that life which is thine, from thee.

Before that we find the entity was in the Holy Land when the Master walked in the earth, when there were those hearings of, not personal experience of, how others were healed by the Master only speaking to them and putting His hand upon the hand, the arm, the head of others.

The entity made fun of — yes, rebuked those — who claimed such had come about; and eventually, when on the day of Pentecost the entity heard and saw the outpouring of the Holy Spirit, it believed and felt it was almost too late.

It is never too late to mend thy ways. For life is eternal and ye are today what ye are because of what ye have been. For ye are the co-creator with thy Maker, that ye may one day be present with all of those who love His coming.

Keep thy faith, then, in the Christ. Do prepare thy body in prayer, in thoughtfulness of others, in patience to thy poor afflicted in thy home, but keep it there.

It is thy problem with thy God, not to be put away until He, who is the giver of life, sees fit to call it home to prepare for the better life that ye have made or may make possible in the gentleness, in thy kindness to thy fellow man.

(5284-1)

A case of muscular dystrophy was also brought to Cayce's attention, and the reading brings to light the karmic nature of the problem, involving the parents as well as their ten-year-old son:

In the present, while these are preventing the abilities of the body to walk, save that as of pushing self through rolling chair, the worry is more with those responsible for the body than with the body itself.

This is a condition of progressive disturbance, more of atrophy of the nerves which control the muscular forces of the body.

Here, as we would find, while the body is meeting itself, those responsible for the body had better be praying for themselves to in attune and to meet conditions (not one, but both).

What was the cause of this condition?

It's meeting its own self. This you won't accept or think, but pray about it and see the difference. This is karma for both the parents and the body.   (5078-1)

Reading 5044-1 was given for a nine-year-old boy but did not provide any details as to his physical abnormality. Counsel was given more for the parents:

In interpreting the physical and mental disturbances here, the sources and basis for these are in the karmic conditions of this body.

To those responsible for this body: Rather than feeling it is a calamity, know that it is an opportunity to meet not only those things in self, but to help this individual entity or soul in its search for its oneness with the Creative Force, or God.

It was during the period of gestation that the condition from the physical standpoint apparently was influenced, but unless there is the activity of those who are responsible for the physical body, the channel through which the soul of this entity is manifested in the present, there may come little help.

Then in patience, in love, in prayer, not in the activities of delegating the care to others, nor of considering it as a burden, but making the administrations as true services, and through the care and love and patience as may be manifested, may ye help, may ye aid, may ye find in the experience that this becomes a pleasure rather than a burden to thy activities.

It will also offer, as indicated, the opportunity of those in the surroundings and environs to learn patience and kindness and gentleness. The body is not to be shunned, but ever treated as an equal, and with all the care that may be made manifest. (5044-1)

The Wet Cell Appliance was advised as treatment for this boy. There is no report as to whether or not it was used.

Again, in the case of 5310, a two-and-a-half-year-old girl, the reading seems to be addressing itself primarily to the parents:

As we find, there is lack of normal development in the mental and the physical forces of the body, lack of true coordination between the cerebrospinal and the sympathetic nervous systems.

These are partially, as we find, in the areas from the conditions existent through the period of gestation and then the soul-entity's meeting itself, or karmic conditions of the entity, as well as those responsible for same.

Help can be had. As to the normalcy being produced, it will depend upon the sincerity in which these suggestions are followed which may be made by those responsible for the entity in the material manifestation.

And each day let the mother, with the father, make those suggestions together, with the body or over the body, as it were; each of them with the hand upon the body as it would sleep, make those prayers, those intercessions as this, in their own words:

"Father, God! In Thy love, in Thy mercy, be thou near unto us in this hour! Heal Thou our hearts, our minds, and the body of this, Thy maid servant. Thy will, O God, be done in each of us! Through Thy promise we ask and seek this help."

This is not to be hurried through with but to be lived day by day.   (5310-1)

Readings 4140 and 3458 also seem to indicate that the greater lesson is for the parents. Certainly the emphasis is on the mental and spiritual attitude of the parents.

Prayer, meditation, together, with, over, for the body, for the spiritual life may be aroused to a greater activity in a developing body by the concerted activity of those that are responsible for its entry into this material plane; but *together!* Do not tempt self, nor that to which ye each would pray.

Why is the child suffering this disharmony in his body?

Meeting those conditions that have been builded, in that which *was* made by self; also answering to that necessary for the activity of the bodies that brought it into being. This may be answered in that as was asked of Him, 'Who sinned that this man was born blind; his parents or this man?' Neither, in that sense, 'but that the glory of God may be made manifest before you.' In this we find the meeting of that condition merited, then, that there may be manifest in the lives of those that might minister to the glory of the Father in His activity in and among men in the earth today!

What is the lesson the parents should learn from this experience?

Patience! For in patience possess ye your souls! (4140-1)

Yes, as we find, conditions here are such that there are lessons to be gained from same, rather than so much that may be accomplished from a physical angle in the present.

These conditions, this soul-entity entering, should be an evidence for the mother, the father, of the fact that life is eternal, and that there will be those as a witness before the throne; that indeed His angel is ever before the throne making intercession for those that are in spirit, in mind, anxious.

Then let the spirit of truth, of light, of hope, enter in.

Do not become hardened. Do not attempt to justify, but let thy life, thy activities ever be such as to glorify that which is held in the heart and in the mind of this body.

That the body entered into this life experience in these disturbed manners, without seeming opportunity, should not allow thee to become hardened. Do not let it cause thee to doubt, but rather be assured that it is a just God, keeping a witness ever before each individual that each may personally know that He cares.

Do that. These attitudes must be in the minds, the hearts, the purposes of the parents in the present. (3458-1)

Coming now to case 3584, we find even more responsibility placed on the parents. For whether the child—a two-year-old boy—would remain in the earth-plane or not depended on the parents' persistence in carrying through with the prescribed treatments. The child's life could be lengthened if the parents desired it. It was up to them.

As we find, there are karmic conditions of the body and also the parents. Yet there are physical disturbances that come from conditions which existed during the period of gestation, and these can be interpreted within themselves if they will analyze it.

These pressures in the brain cells, from the portion of the central gland through which and from which the life processes begin, caused at the time of presentation, pressures in the head and neck.

The days in the present may be materially lengthened, but the response will depend upon whether or not those responsible wish to carry through with this or to let processes of nature or time disintegrate this body from the entity or soul.

There may be somewhat of a response, and this may be better accomplished (should there be the desire to keep the life here) by the direct application of the low electrical forces that may be had from the Abrams Machine [reference to a device developed by Dr. Albert Abrams, for supposedly measuring and modifying the electro-magnetic waves in a human body] or this low energy to the body, which would carry the life-forces. Massages should be given along with this. (3584-1)

In yet another situation of abnormalcy, we have a case of arrested development in a child. The answer to a question submitted by the parents is of interest here:

Is this condition peculiar to this child alone; that is, can the mother expect that any other child she may have will be normal?

As just indicated, this is a condition to this entity. Any other child the mother may have, may have the chance to be normal. (3143-1)

Despite the answer, however, it had been indicated elsewhere in the reading that the situation was karmic. It was *not* a "happenstance"!

A speech defect was involved in the case of a 14-year-old boy, and was ascribed to karmic causes in which the parents apparently had a part:

As we find disturbances here indicate—as they are active principles through the sensory organisms of the body and the sensory system—an incoordination between the impulses, the brain reflexes, and the spiritual forces of the body.

Thus the condition is karmic in its reaction.

Those who are responsible for the body-physical need not feel that this responsibility can be delegated to some-

93.

one else, even though others may be physically better able to cope with or to train the body for its present conditions.

These disturbances might be helped if there would be the daily prayer together of those responsible for the body; not one day and then skip one, but each day for a period of three hundred sixty-five days. As the body goes to sleep let those responsible for the body-physical meet over the body, or with the body, and in prayer make suggestions to the body as it sleeps.

True this should have been begun six years ago but it still may aid.

Do not begin unless there is sincerity in both parents of this entity.

Otherwise, let others give that instruction, that help—for the body is meeting itself; but so must those responsible for this entity meet themselves.   (4013-1)

Is it not becoming increasingly evident, as we review these cases of abnormalcy in children, that the karmic causal patterns are most frequently mutual between the parents and the child? At the very least, some immutable law of reciprocity appears to be involved in the incoming soul-entity's choice of a specific human channel for its expression. The meeting of self, in other words, may often require a given cast of characters! And each member of the cast is called upon to play out his or her role on the stage of life, lest the performance be pronounced a failure.

Even when the parents are not directly involved in the karma of the child, as was the situation in the next case for our consideration, the parents appear to have been specifically chosen because they were apparently best able to perform a necessary act of love and service on behalf of that particular, troubled soul-entity, and to the glory of God.

A young man of nineteen was physically helpless and entirely dependent on others. The reading Cayce gave for him revealed that this was karma accrued during a life of wantonness and selfishness. Here, first, is an extract of a letter from the boy's aunt, dated July 23, 1940, to Cayce:

I am most anxious for a reading of my nephew, 19 years old. He is a little unfortunate child whom medical science has been unable to help, and while we dare not hope to have him attain normalcy in this life, it would be a great comfort to his mother to KNOW the causes leading up to this karma, and to know if there is ANYTHING she should do or COULD do to help him, more than she has already. Naturally, IF there could be a cure—anything you would suggest would be done.

The reading follows:

In giving the interpretations of the records as we find them here, much of this information would be most beneficial to all who disregard counsel (and advice) as to their mental and spiritual relationships to their fellow men through material sojourns.

All might take a lesson, or learn something of the mercies of the Father to those who in their ignorance disregard others yet seek a way ever—as each soul does—to know their relationships one to another, and to creative or God-forces.

Here we find a physical expression of wantonness and selfishness manifested, in the lack of the mental and spiritual expression in the present—save through constant care upon the part of others.

Well might any questions come to the mother, the parents, as to why and how this must be a part of their experience in this material sojourn.

Well that each remember, it is LAW; and that only in Him—who hath fulfilled the law, replacing it with mercy, love, hope and understanding—can such be wholly comprehended or understood.

It is not always the sin of the parents that such be their measure of responsibility, but of it is as here—rather that the soul-consciousness of this entity may become aware of what true abiding love leads individuals to do concerning those who are wholly dependent upon others for every care; thus fulfilling, thus completing a full understanding of that law.

So easily it is misinterpreted, so oft passed over as being beautiful but not applicable in thy own experience!

But to all here we see same manifested in a material way and manner, namely—'As ye do it unto the least of these, my brethern, ye do it unto me,' saith the Lord.

So, with what measure ye mete—in body, in mind, in spirit—the same is measured to thee.

The fulfilling of such in the experience of the parents, of the entity itself, makes same null and void in the experience as sin. For the Lord loveth those who repent. For there is the more joy over the one that returns than the ninety and nine just that never strayed away.

So, it was for—it is through, it is by such love that has been manifested and is being manifested in the experience of this entity, that he entered this particular environ.

As was manifested in the experience of Him—though He were without sin, He offered His body, His blood, His life, that we through Him might have the access to the Father of light, of love, of hope, of mercy.

Thus we find here an entity who in the appearances and experiences before this knew of—yea, in many of those sojourns was well acquainted with—those who did kindnesses, those who patiently and lovingly did minister to the needs of those who were without hope, who were disturbed in body and in mind as to which way to turn and as to what courses to pursue. Yet the entity turned away from same, that there might be the joys of the material nature, the enjoying of appetites in self for a season.

Yet here we find the entity is overtaken, and that what

the entity has sown he is reaping. These conditions, then, bring opportunities for those who minister, those who care for such, to meet their own selves—in joy or in duty, obligation.

With love did the Father offer His Son. With love, patience and understanding did the Son give what will be the measure of faith of those who minister here to this soul—who is entering into an awakening through that being administered in the present.

Let the periods of attaching this [Radio-active] Appliance be used as periods when suggestion would be made to the mental and physical beings, by those responsible for the care of—for the life flow of blood in this experience.

Doing this in faith, in hope, much may be accomplished as time (as ye call it) passes.

But do this in that manner even as He administered, knowing ye may only sow the seed of truth, of hope, of mercy, of kindness, of patience, and let God give the increase; leaving it with Him.   (2319-1)

Epilepsy

There are about 100 cases of epilepsy in the Edgar Cayce readings.

It is of interest that the statement was made in some instances that the sins of the father were being visited upon the child. Since we tend to keep family associations throughout the ages, even to being the reincarnation of one of our own ancestors occasionally, epilepsy is a dis-ease pattern which offers food for thought.

Here are excerpts from several cases in the Cayce files:

Here we have conditions where there may be the blame physically upon the indiscretion of the father. In reality it is the combination of self meeting self, and still the physical indiscretion of the parent.   (3430-1)

97.

As we find, there are conditions that disturb the physical, the mental, and the soul entity. This we find is a prenatal condition; and must be met by the body as well as by those responsible for the body.

It should not be delegated too oft, then, to someone else to administer those influences in the body-physical or mental for the correction of the disturbance.   (3156-1)

Please give the mother of the child some advice that may help her in aiding, and rearing the child.

As indicated, this must be a spiritual awakening. Not that there may be said, Do this or Do that, but the desire must be created in the innate and manifested activities by accepting and doing that which is in keeping with the spiritual forces as manifested in the Christ.   (2139-1)

It is rather unfortunate that only a relatively limited number of people, out of the many hundreds who came to Cayce for physical readings in connection with various disease patterns, sought life readings, as well. This prevents us from being able to conduct a meaningful comparison study between specific diseases and their karmic causal forces, as revealed in former earth experiences, or actions, to which the present physical disturbances, or dis-eases, are attributed.

In the case of epilepsy, however, we do find a number of instances in which life readings were also sought, and these tend to suggest a repetitive pattern. The source of the trouble was almost invariably traceable to overindulgence and misuse of the reproductive forces, or the sexual function, in a prior life. The creative forces, it would seem, cannot be abused with impunity.

The present and previous parental relationships of a twelve-year-old girl, who was having epileptic seizures, is an interesting case. Her parents, who were also involved in this karma, were the same as in a previous earth experience. She was told that her condition came from a life at the time of the

American Revolution.   Readings given for her parents indicated that they had used their daughter to obtain information. Not only did she use *psychic* energy for this purpose, but she excited physical fires and used sex for this purpose.

Those responsible for this entity as an individual expression of a soul in this experience, should parallel their experiences showing those opportunities and those obligations with this entity.   For, with such a paralleling (through their own life readings, you see), there would be a much greater comprehension of purposes as come into the experiences of those who oft are inclined to pass off such disturbances as chance, or as conditions that are unavoidable.

Yet each soul as it visions the experiences, the hardships in the experience of this entity, should realize that indeed each soul meets itself, and God is not mocked but whatsoever a soul soweth, that shall it also reap.

On the other hand, the relationships through the material or earthly sojourns may give a vision of the self, and self-aggrandizements or indulgences that find their expression in a physical condition in the experience of an individual entity who also is reaping that of its own whirlwind.

Hence as we find, as to the appearances of this entity:

Before this the entity was in the land of the present nativity, but closer to those activities about the founding or settling of the land.

Then as Marjorie Desmond, the entity was active in the associations with many, as to relationships which excited the fires of the physical being of many.

Thus the inability in the present of coordinating the emotions with the mental attributes.

But, as indicated, those who are now responsible for the entrance of the entity into this material plane were those who were then responsible in the greater measure for the lack of exercising due consideration to the activities, and allowed same in measures for the greater material gains. Consequently, they, too, in the present are meeting much that may be overcome in this experience.

Before that the entity was in the Promised Land, at those periods of the return of the children of promise to the rebuilding of the city, the temple, and the walls thereof.

The entity then was among those close in the household of those who directed that activity, under the direct lineage of Zerubbabel, of the Levites—and this of those of the priesthood.

In the beginnings the entity aided much, but with the disputations which arose regarding others who were descendents of those left in the land, the entity aided more with those; and thus brought distrubing forces in its experience, and that rebellion which again found expression in the material environs in that sojourn just previous to the present sojourn, which we have just indicated.

The name then was Esdreldia.

Before that the entity was in the lands when there were the journeyings from the house or land of bondage to the free land, or the land of promise.

The entity then also was of the lineage of the Levites, but of the Korah tribe—being among the daughters of the son of Korah.

In that experience the entity gained, and yet held to its duty to its father and mother, which brought destructive experiences in the activities of the entity in its youth; though the entity was not destroyed when those of the household of Korah were destroyed. However, resentments were builded in a manner that found expression again, without due consideration to the spiritual experiences of the entity.

Thus the necessity in the present—for the TRUTH of spiritual life and spiritual processes as related to the material *and* mental forces—for the entity returning to a physical, mental and spiritual understanding in order for there to be a normal balance.

The name then was Ashbahel.

Before that the entity was in the Egyptian land, among the offspring of the Atlanteans, though born and reared to activity in the Egyptian experience for the developments towards establishing what is now known as the hospitalization of individual's ills of body or mind, and the segregations of activities or influences that are within themselves detrimental or undermining to the physical and mental well-being of individuals.

Thus we find the entity in the present innately appreciates those things pertaining to vibrations as in music; and these will be helpful forces in not only the suggestive but the active forces of the body in the present; also things pertaining to helpful influences in the experiences of others.

As to that to which the entity may attain, and how:

As indicated, this depends much upon the attitudes and applications of those who may use influences to restore, renew and bring about a better physical balance within the experience of the entity.

And then in the training pertaining to those things indicated through which it has gained in the material sojourns, may the outlet come for greater experiences for this entity.

Has the condition of the body for the past ten years had any effect upon it physically and mentally?

Necessarily, these have not been—nor are they yet—co-ordinated.

What type of education should body have to prepare her for life?

The musical education, as indicated, as well as the inclination towards that of nursing.

Any particular musical instrument you would suggest?

Any that have the *vibrations* as created in the environs of the body.

101.

What effect has destiny on the present appearances?

This depends, as indicated, upon the application of those who have brought the entity into its present environs; and the greater *destiny* may be according to how well there is the application of the obligations due the entity.

What will aid her to overcome her physical and mental ailments?

As indicated, the physical exertions, exercises and activities for the body.   (2153-3)

The parents were advised to be careful of this girl's diet; that it was a very important part of her treatment. They were also told to avoid giving her sedatives, though it might become necessary at times.

In a later reading, further counsel was given for her general care, including the medically interesting suggestion to give her salt. In reading 2153-7, there were words of encouragement. This reading stated that her condition was improving, and the parents were told that she would be healed.

Meanwhile, the parents' readings give us futher information on their responsibility and involvement with their daughter during her life in America in Revolutionary times.

From the father's reading:

Before this the entity was in those lands nigh unto that land of the present nativity, during those early activities of the American Revolution.

Then the entity was halted between two ways oft; as to whether to choose the cause of the colonists or to remain with the King—or that belief.

Thus we find those periods of confusion were brought about by the attempts of the entity and his companion to gather data and information for the use of those whom the entity felt were in authority.

These, in the associations of one in the home at present,

brought destructive forces in the beginning; but with those realizations that there were real unseen forces being made manifest, there came the period of spiritual awakening.

However, the misuse of those privileges brings material disturbances in the present; but faith and hope and spiritual application may bring again those things that may make the realization that He *is* a God of love, and loves those who repent—though each soul must meet its *own* self.

The name then was Elisha Desmond. In that experience the entity lost, the entity gained; and throughout the period there were fears of what others would say—and these have been a part of the experience in the present.

Rather know that the life, the associations, the activities with others bespeak of those that are as the ideals of the entity. For, greater is the voice of those whom the entity has favored—or to whom he has shown brotherly love, kindness, gentleness, patience, long-suffering—than the voice of praise of those who have their own ends to attain. For, such as indicated are the seed of the spirit of truth; and in doing those, being those, fear not as to what others may say. For, if the Lord be with thee, *who* can be against thee?

And now, from the mother's reading:

Before this the entity was among those who were kept in a state of disturbance by the very relationships with the conditions which surrounded the activities of the settlers, and their relationships with the conditions surrounding them in regard to the Revolutionary period.

The entity's part, with the companion, in ruling over the abilities of one (now the daughter) for the insight or seership, brought fear and doubt in self as to the authenticity of same; and the desire to make same practical and material brought disturbing experiences.

And these may be met in the present experience—indeed must be met; for these are innate. Look rather to that admonition given of old, in the 30th and 31st of Deuteronomy, as to where and how *all* such are to be met—*within,* through the seeking to know His will with thee.

The entity lost and the entity gained through that experience.

For, with the changes wrought, and the periods of reconstruction with the companion's activities in that having to do with household effects, as well as conditions in relationship to the exports and imports, we find that greater opportunities were brought; and the entity found His way as applicable in the experience with others.

The name then was Leigh Desmond.　　(2344-1)

Another case of epilepsy, involving the indiscretions of the parents, has biblical overtones:

The entity, were it able—will it arouse within self that that will be able to subdue the passions of those influences which have become inherent from the indiscretions of the youth of the parents of the entity—there will be brought the full knowledge and understanding that the truth *in* Him makes one free indeed, and though the law says that, 'I will visit the afflictions of the fathers upon the children to the third and fourth generation,' so also is that healing and that balm in Gilead as comes through the gift of the Son *into* the world, that 'Though thy sins be as scarlet they shall be white like wool.'　　(543-11)

In case 693, we have an example of karma brought over from the Salem period. The child, in the present experience, was not wanted; and one might speculate that one of the other of the parents—perhaps both—could have been among those who were belittled and victimized by this person in his Salem incarnation, although the reading does not say so. At any rate, it seems that he had physically abused, for sexual gratification, some of those who were apparently accused of witchcraft and persecuted.

Yet oft, as we find here, individuals again and again are drawn together that there may be the meeting in the experience of each that which will make them aware of wherein they, as individuals (individual entity and soul), have erred respecting experiences in materiality or soul life even. For the soul lives on, and unless that which has been the trouble, the barrier, the dissenting influence in the experience is met in self's relationships to Creative Forces, it must gradually make for deteriorating experiences in the expression of such a spirit influence in matter—or materiality.

In this entity we find it coming under the influence of these things rather in the earth, that have made for that which in the flesh and in the mental forces makes for those expressions of conditions that must not only be met *by* self but in those who *have* been and are responsible for the entering of the soul into the experience. O that men (or man) would become cognizant of the necessity of preparations within themselves for being the channels for giving a soul the opportunity for expressions in the earth, or in matter! *This* soul, or this *body*, was not wanted; yet as it came with those surrounding environs, those attitudes and those wishes and those desires that made for the entrance, we have that which must be met. As we find, if those things are adhered to in a conscientious manner that we have indicated, much of that may be eradicated by the time there are those periods [adolescence] when the alterations or changes come in the activative influences within the body itself. If it is allowed to become a portion of the developing manhood and the expression of same into materiality, less and less will there be the opportunity for the eradicating of same entirely from the system.

As to the expressions of the entity in the earth, we find:

Before this it was in those environs, in the land now known as Salem, and the experience about Providence Town when there were the expressions and activities that made for the suppression of individuals in meeting those experiences that came as the expressions of spiritual manifestations in the experiences of others.

The entity was not only among those that made for the belittling of such but induced the material activity in the suppression, in the expression; and not only took advantage of that that were being oppressed but used same in such a manner to gratify, satisfy, the passions of the body in associations with same. These made for the expressions that have brought in the experience of the entity in the present that which makes for the more often the attempt of expression of self during that sojourn, or during that experience; and almost a possession takes place within the body when there are those touchings upon those things when the *mind* of the body attempts to rest, such that others creep close to the border; making for those manifestations that bring into the experience the uncontrollableness within its own self. Yet much of that which may make for the corrections in same lies within those abilities of those that are responsible for its physical entrance in the present. (693-3)

A very severe case, and a quite sad one. The lust to control and dominate other people in one lifetime damaged the physical system of a subsequent one, producing epilepsy. At the outset, the boy seemed to improve; but the epileptic seizures returned, later on, with full severity. The recommended treatment emphasized the need for earnest prayer and spiritual attunement. Judging by the mother's description of the boy's pathetic condition, one wonders how it would have been possible for the child's soul, if it had been reached through prayer, to have had much healing impact.

There were other cases of karmic epilepsy, however, which were apparently cured. At least, following a lapse of several years between followup reports, there had been no recurrence of the seizures.

The recommended treatment, in most cases, was fairly simple. But it required a lot of time, patience and persistence; no swift recoveries were promised. This may have proved discouraging to many, who were obviously hoping for faster results. But it is in patience, we are told, that we possess our souls. And apparently the karmic pattern typically associated with epilepsy was of such a nature that it normally required an extended period of time, coping patiently with this rather grotesque and frightening handicap, in order for the entity (and, sometimes, the parents too!) to face self and reap what had been sown. Yet one's degree of suffering need only be sufficient to regenerate the soul.

Multiple Sclerosis

Among the victims of multiple sclerosis, one case is found in the Cayce material in which the individual, although he did not have a life reading, was told that his dis-ease was of karmic origin. It is a particularly instructive case, so we present it here in some detail. The story commences with these excerpts from a follow-up letter to Edgar Cayce, dated October 18, 1943, from Sarah Robertson, an attendent nurse:

[This is one] of the most emotional and self-centered people that I have ever known. You say that I must help him to see that he needs spiritual food as well as physical help. I have tried, Mr. Cayce, but I don't think I have succeeded very well. He is touchy and close-mouthed, and will say, "Don't let's talk about it. It is too deep a matter." I can't tell whether he feels a great deal, or not at all, except a burning desire to be physically whole again. We can't *force* a person to see spiritual values by talking about it. That is one reason I have assumed the responsibility of continuing to do for him, though his lack of consideration to me (and others who are trying to help him) and his egotism have nearly worn me out. I want to *prove* to him, and so do others here, that the principle of Christian love and service is above just personal feelings. There is much involved in this whole affair.

I leave in a week or two....I will try to keep in touch with you, and tell you all I know. This young man believes in you, or says he does, and I think your influence will count more than anything I can say or do.

And here, in the words of the patient himself, is some background data he furnished at the time he requested his first physical reading:

Before I was married, I had a mysterious attack of some kind which made me practically blind for a year, and which no doctor was able to diagnose. At the end of a year, with no medical assistance, the condition cleared up and I was about as well as before the attack. Some time after I was married and my son was about two years old, the trouble with my eyes returned, plus a general disability of my legs and arms. My trouble has been diagnosed as multiple sclerosis. Medical science seems to know little of this condition and holds out no hope for me.

In accordance with the request, a physical reading was given:

Here we find conditions advanced in multiple sclerosis, so-called, or the inability of the digestive forces and the glands in the liver (in the right lobe) to supply those tendencies needed, or energies needed, to supply the return force in nerve energy.

As is understood by some, thought by many, there is within each physical being the elements whereby the organs and their activities and functionings are enabled within themselves to supply that needed for replenishing or rebuilding their own selves.

This may be done, as comprehended, in a period of every seven years. Thus it is a slow process, but it is a growth in the energies of the body and thus necessitates there being kept a normal balance in the chemistry of the body-force itself. For it is either from potash, iodine, soda or fats, that each of these in their various combinations and multiple activities supply all the other forces of the body-energies. Yet in each body there is born or projected that something of the soul-self also.

Thus we find what is commonly called the law of cause and effect, or karmic conditions being met by an individual entity. For, as given of old, each soul shall give an account of every idle word spoken. It shall pay every whit. And this is as self-evident as the statement, 'In the day ye eat thereof ye shall surely die.' It is as demonstrative as, 'Be ye fruitful, and multiply, subdue the earth.'

This entity, then, is still at war with itself, but all hate, all malice, all that would make man afraid, must be eliminated, first from the mind of the individual entity. And he knows, should know, there is an advocate with the Father. For, as was given to that one called to be the leader of his people, 'Who maketh thy tongue? Who maketh thine eyes to see, thine ears to hear, thine feet to walk?' Is it not the Lord?

Hence, He has given in the earth that which, when sought by the individual entity or soul that acknowledges it has gone astray, helps to meet whatever condition that may have come to pass. For, as given, 'Though ye wander far, if ye call I will hear, and answer speedily.'

And this may be you, if you will but hearken. But if you turn your face away, know there is not in heaven or hell that which may separate you from the love of God—as He has promised in His word—but yourself. And others seek

109.

to help you, as we would here, if you will but listen.

Then, right about *face! Know* that the Lord liveth, and would do thee good—if ye will but trust wholly in Him!

There are pathological conditions indicated, or those indicating that the body-forces have refused to respond. But there are elements in the earth that may aid you in gaining the control. For, who makes the sun to shine? Who gives the bitterness to quinine? Who gives the sweetness to sugar? Is it man, because he found it? Or was it put there by the Maker in the beginning, for man to find and to use in its proper place and relationship to his associations one with another? To meet the needs of a physical being, either in pleasure or in displeasure with those influences which have been too much absorbed in self?

Here we find there is lacking in the body those elements that may be supplied through chloride of gold sodium, by the use of the low vibrations as they may be added to the body in such measures that the organs deficient may use them in their assimilation to strengthen the nerve supply and add to the nerve plasm that is lacking in giving stamina and strength to the nerves of the legs, of the body, yes of the whole being.

Making thy heart right, making attunement with that golden harp of life, let it play upon thine own imagination as to how ye will use thyself to the glory of God, to the love of thy fellow man—if there is given that power within. For, lo, as He has promised, 'Look not to heaven nor overseas, for Lo, it is within thine own self that ye may know thy God to do His biddings.'

At this juncture, the reading advised treatment with massage and the use of the Wet Cell Appliance.

It then continued:

This will not be a hurried response, but in less than three months you should see the change—if you expect it, and if those administering the treatments are conscientious, consistent, faithful and purposeful.

Do these things, if we would find betterment.   (3124-1)

Later, this individual became totally blind. A second reading calls attention to his attitude. Certainly this particular reading is counseling holistic healing. The young man needed to change his attitudes and become less selfish. Moreover, he was told that he had to seek God and become attuned to the Divine within, or the Christ Presence, if he would be helped. There was even an intimation that his motive in seeking a healing was to be free again to resume former bad habits. Here are excerpts from that reading:

There have been physical improvements in the body, yet there is much, much to be desired.

As indicated for the body, this is a karmic condition and there must be measures taken for the body to change its attitude towards conditions, things and its fellow men.

So long as there were those practical applications of the mechanical things for physical correction, and there were those concerted efforts on the part of the body's friends to make intercession in prayer, improvements were indicated.

When the body becomes so self-satisfied, so self-centered as to renounce, refuse, or does not change its attitude, so long as there is hate, malice, injustice, those things that produce hate, those that produce jealousy, those that produce that which is at variance to patience, long-suffering, brotherly love, kindness, gentleness, there cannot be healing to that condition of this body.

As first indicated, what would the body be healed for? That it might gratify its own physical appetites? That it might add to its own selfishness? Then (if so) it had better remain as it is.

If there is the change in mind, in intent, in purpose, and the body expresses same in its speech, its acts, and there is the application of those things suggested in the manners suggested, we will find improvement.

But first the change of heart, the change of mind, the change of purpose, the change of intent.

If these are done, then keep the massages also. But don't be so selfish or so self-centered that there is the imagination that others will not respond. If ye show thyself friendly, ye will find friends. Will ye pray, will ye ask God and Christ to forgive thee? Will ye forgive others? For it is only as ye forgive that even the Savior, the Christ, is able to forgive thee. But if ye forgive it will be double to thee in thy abilities, in thy activities, in thy improvements.

Do use the appliance that has been suggested, consistently. Yes, it carries those elements that are material. But what is the spirit of gold? What is the spirit of any element that has life-giving influence in itself? Is it of thine own making or is there not the power within as was given from the beginning? It has always remained there, for it is of the first cause of life, the Word, the principle; that which may be made thine if ye turn to Him who is the Life, who is the Light, who is thy Savior—if ye will but accept Him.

All of the mechanical appliances that ye may muster will not aid to complete recovery *unless* thy purpose, unless thy soul has been baptized with the Holy Spirit.

In Him, then, is thy hope. Will ye reject it? He offers, 'Today—if ye will hearken, if ye will but listen, if ye will but begin to apply love, hope, faith, forgiveness.' Then may ye indeed be washed in the blood of the Lamb that taketh away the sin of the world—thy world. Thy body is indeed the temple of the living God. And what does it appear in the present? Broken in purpose, broken in the ability to reproduce itself! What is lacking? That which is life itself, which is of and is the manifestation of the influence or force ye call God, that is God in manifestation.

Will ye accept, will ye reject? It is up to thee.   (3124-2)

He did order the material for the Wet Cell Appliance. We do not know, however, how long he may have used it, if at all, or of its effectiveness. There is no follow-up report in the files on this case.

The next reading on multiple sclerosis is for another young man whose attitudes and activities were materialistic and self-indulgent, in a carryover from past lives. His present condition signaled a need, now, to mend his ways. If healing was to be accomplished, there had to be a change in the mental and spiritual attitudes and ideals.

Yes, we have the body and those conditions physically, and that attitude mentally which has hindered and does hinder in the application of those things that might be helpful in the present; also those conditions that hinder the better physical manifestations through this body.

As to the approach this body is making in the present, first we find that the body should analyze self, self's own attitude to the conditions that surround the body; those things from the mental and the material aspects that have hindered and do hinder—and we will find that much of this has been and is of the nature that from self-indulgences in the present, in the past, there has been brought into the experience of the entity those things that may and must be accorded in self, as to the usefulness, the purposefulness, those active desires for the body to make a regeneration within self sufficiently that—if there are to be brought about within the physical forces of the body itself that which would make for the abilities for the body to cope with conditions—the body may act under those influences wherein there has not as yet been the activity within self *as to not condemn someone else.* For those influences that have made for the blames for this, that and the other experience, have come about that are mostly of thine own making! Yet what would be accomplished within self if there were made those things in the physical forces that would make for the abilities for the body to meet and match with those influences about it, to wrest from the manifested influences and forces about the body that would make for its equaling, that which would make for its comparing of self and self's abilities with those of its fellow man? *What* would be thine own attitude, then?

Again, would the body bring onto self those things that would only answer for, and make for the activities within its own associations that would make for the aggrandizement of self's own interests? Or would the body rather merit and meet its spiritual aptitude such as to use its abilities in a service for its fellow man? Would it give of itself? Not in its own way, but in the way that the divine influences would guide—that come into the experience of each and every soul, that must be met within the heart and within the aptitude of the individual itself; for its own soul's development, the soul being that portion of every individual and every entity that must live on—and on—and on!

Then, if the attitude of self to those conditions and experiences through which the entity is passing in the present continues to make for this condemnation—with the wreck that is made within the body itself, and the little responses that are made to those influences from without—how must these be met?

Only first, then, if the body will make for that determination, that concentration, the *consecration* of its manner of *thinking*, into and through those influences that may be accorded within self, *then* may there be able to be given— through such channels as these—that which may bring for the body that which may be helpful and hopeful, for that determination. And it is what measure ye mete that it may be measured to thee again, as to those influences and forces within self. *Then* may we meet those conditions within self that have made for, do make for, the inroads upon the physical activities—in the overtautness in portions of the system, where there has been the deviation from those influences that make for production of an even coordination through a physical body; that may be used as for making the world itself—its environs, its surroundings, its *own* associations—a better place for the entity having lived in same!

What, you ask then, are the physical conditions that are disturbing the forces of the body? These are evident within themselves from the physical conditions that are shown in the various portions of the system. Has the body sought?

If the body physically and mentally seeks for self, or that it may become a greater, a better, a more nominal channel through which the abilities—the birthright, the soul—may manifest for the glorification of the creative energies or forces that are manifested in the life of every living object, condition, experience or soul or body, *then* we may aid.

(716-1)

Eleven months later, a second physical reading was obtained:

While there might be much given as to that which has caused or produced the conditions, these should be rather viewed by the entity in this attitude: 'The physical conditions that have come upon me are those most necessary for my soul's development.' While there have been periods of antagonism and of belittling self, making for the berating of the circumstance, the conditions that have come upon self, know that these conditions have given thee the opportunity to see that in it all there has been given the privilege for others to express in their activity the true spirit of love, that creative influence that is worshipped by man as God. And these in thine own self and in thine own mind, in thine own body, then, can quicken that which will make for thine own self, thine

115.

own body, thine own mind, being and manifesting that same influence in the lives of those that thou may meet, that thou may contact day by day. Yea, they may bring to thee—with thine own inspiration, thine *own* intuitive forces, by applying them in thine own experience—such creative influences, such creative energies, as to *renew* thy strength. For His promises have been given: 'Those that love me will I renew, even as the strength of the unicorn, as the flight of the eagle, and thy days and thy habitation shall be called blessed by those that know thee.' (716-2)

A third reading enjoined the impatient sufferer to practice greater patience:

Yes, we have the body here, and this we have had before.

Now, as we find, there are not the indications outwardly of an improvement in any *perceptible* manner. Yet, with the application of those things indicated (that is, with the rubs, with the appliance, with the activities physically and mentally), there *is* being brought about that which has been *helpful*. And if the body loses patience with self, then that which has been indicated for the body is not to be the proper direction taken!

But there should be the persistence; for the conditions have been—as has been given—not only of long duration but there have been the attempts on the part of the body physically and mentally to *adjust* itself to the deficiencies that have existed!

Give the TIME! Be PATIENT! You've had years and *years* of the disturbance. Don't expect it to be cured in a moment and be of a permanent nature. For the body, the life, the whole of every entity *is* a GROWTH; and unless it is of such a growth that is stable, it isn't worth very much!

Be patient. Be consistent. Be persistent. Follow those suggestions that *have* been made. And we will find help.

We are through with this reading. (716-3)

In a letter to this fellow's father, dated January 12, 1935, Edgar Cayce wrote, in part: "Tell him that I would like to keep a check-up on his condition every three or four weeks, for I am most anxious that he gets those things suggested. I realize that it may require time and patience in his case, but it has been of long standing and that necessary most is the right way of thinking and acting about everything."

A reply from the father, six days later, raised some questions about the treatments. Mr. Cayce sent detailed instructions on January 22, augmenting the specifics already outlined in the readings as to dosages, rubs, and so forth. There were no further communications from the young man or his father. On November 12, 1936—almost two years later—Mr. Cayce wrote directly to the youth, inquiring about his condition, but there was no reply.

This next case of multiple sclerosis is an intriguing one. Apparently the person, in an earlier incarnation in America, meted out harsh and savage punishment to others "in the struggle for freedom on the part of some with whom the entity joined." Now, in his physical body in the present, he was reaping the results of his earlier cruelty, which had rendered many helpless:

Before this, then, the entity was in the land of the present sojourn, in those associations with the activities in the struggle for freedom on the part of some with whom the entity joined; yet the mercilessness of the savage (as would be termed in the present) was indicated in the orders given by the entity in dealing with characters and activities.

And these rendered many helpless. Ye are meeting same in thine own self. And some of those upon whom ye meted those measures must today measure to thee in patience.

Thus gain ye in that experience, through knowing as ye sow, that must ye reap. For, life—the manifestation of that power, that influence ye call God—is continuous; and self must be purged that ye may walk as one with Him.

(2564-3)

The counsel given in these next two cases is very instructive. In the one instance, we find a warning against letting fear creep in, which can then lead to resignation. In the second, the entity is given spiritual encouragement, pointing the way to resuscitating the life force "in each cellular unit of the body," until finally "there may be added many days yet of a *useful* service in the vineyard of thy Maker."

Yes—such a lovely person!

As we find, the conditions here are a combination of the karmic as well as of a physical condition neglected in the body.

These have produced multiple sclerosis, and it has advanced to such an extent that it becomes something to deal with.

As we find, this may be retarded, possibly not eliminated; but will depend much upon how consistent and persistent the body may be in having the administrations made.

For, with the lack of ability of locomotion, and the *fear* that has entered with it—and then resignation—all have their combined effect upon the expectancies of the mental and spiritual body; with hopes, yet without something to tie that hope to.

And the results will depend upon patience, time, and the attitudes of the body.

But don't lose the hold on self nor its abilities to ever be a helpful influence in the lives of those who come in contact with you, for the glory of the divine within!   (3041-1)

Yes, we have the body here.

Now, while conditions are rather serious, they are long

standing, and the condition has become progressive, we find that, with a great deal of care and patience, and persistence, the body may be able to care for itself—and to engage in activities that would be more in keeping with its purposes for entering this material plane.

First, the attitudes of the body must be considered. While at times there have been hopes, these have gradually faded; and the body has at many times become very antagonistic to all that would pertain to a spiritual or mental attitude that would be helpful.

Resignation to the conditions does not necessarily mean patience on the part of the body. Know, deep within self, that God is not mocked. And while to self in the present these conditions may not appear to be results of thine own self—whose body is afflicted? Thy body is indeed the temple of the living God. What manner of worship hast gone on, then, in the real body? Not the physical being, that at present is hindered by pathological conditions, illnesses, lack of the ability of locomotion, lack of the activity of the organs that function to bring the physical conditions for carrying on, and the ability to reproduce themselves in themselves.

For, each anatomical structure, each atom, each vibration of each organ, must be able to rebuild itself—if there will be the returning of the elements for its recuperation to any extent.

There must be created—in mind, in purpose, in body—those influences and forces that will resuscitate life itself in each cellular unit of the body.

These activities must begin within self as for a purpose, as for hope, as for desire. Not as boastful, not as egotistical, but that each word, each act, each hope, each element of activity, is to be selfless and unto the glory of Creative Forces, or God.

If this, then, becomes to the body as but sounding brass, forget it!

But, know, He *is* the giver of life. He *is* life, in thee. And if there is the seeking, if there is the belief, if there is the *acting*—in mind, in body—to *subdue* the earth, the material disturbances—there may be added many days yet of a *useful* service in the vineyard of thy Maker, to the glory of thy Brother, the Christ; who gave Himself that ye might have intercession with the Father, through just such circumstances in body and mind as have overtaken thee in the present.

That is the beginning, then; thy attitude.

In the physical, then, we have many changes that are to be wrought. Many of those things that have become dormant are to become active again, through the limbs, through the nerves, through the activities of the organs to coordinate with the life plasm itself that keeps the body-entity alive, that makes the body even aware—not only of its physical disability but of regrets, the feelings of imposition upon the activities and the goodness and the grace and the mercy and the love of those *for* whom the body finds it would like to do, itself.

How, then, may the physical applications be brought about? These will require that there be daily attention, not only to this attitude that has been indicated.

And search ye the scriptures daily. For in them ye have promises that are *thine!* In them ye have hope. In them ye have the promise of life, of eternal life, of the water of life, of the bread of life, that makes man free; free here and now—of disease, of disturbance in the various centers of those conditions where the lack of the activity of the liver in itself has taken from the body-forces those influences that will add to the nerve and muscular forces of the body the stamina, the strength.

But these are present in the earth through the application, then, in love, in patience, in persistence, in *using* that thou hast daily in hand, and the next step may be given thee.

And most of all, keep that attitude indicated. And study the Book—to show thyself approved unto Him.

Pray daily; not for self, but to be used as a channel of manifestation of the mercy of God; that ye may glorify Him—not man, not others, but glorify God as manifested in the Christ. (2994-1)

Parkinson's Disease

Parkinson's disease is a disorder of the nervous system in which a deep part of the brain, the substantia nigra, is damaged. People with this disease are deficient in brain dopamine, producing such symptoms as cog-wheel rigidity, tremors, and very slow voluntary movements. It often develops 20 to 50 years following a severe viral infection of the brain, and is sometimes a complication of the use of mind-altering drugs—especially tranquilizers. There seem to be various physical stages, or developing symptoms, which finally result in the manifestation of this disease. Case 1471 provides insight as to what we consider to be the real or inner cause of this condition. The other cases, which follow, offer additional understanding of this degenerative disorder, also pointing out the effect upon the glandular system.

As we find, in giving that as may be helpful for this particular body, many of the physical conditions as well as the mental attitudes must be taken into consideration—if the applications of that as we find might be helpful would be applied in that spirit of cooperative forces in bringing relief.

The conditions have been rather a growth; that is, hindrances that through negative thought as well as sometimes negative reactions have allowed some of the disturbances to become as a constitutional condition.

Hence these must be taken into consideration in the manner in which these have affected and do affect the functioning of the organs of the body itself.

121.

It is very true that *mind* is the control, mind is the builder, and mind may be made wholly a spiritual force or source. Yet remember these as related to a physical being work through a physical organism, in every atom of which there are energies as within themselves.

Hence often there are the needs, as we find in this particular condition, that there be the application of the mechanical means as well as the influence that will work directly upon the functioning of the system as related to the physical body.

True, the active principles even of these—must be in their *essence* of a creative nature or force; else they become not coordinant with the activities of the mental and spiritual forces of the body.   (1471-1)

The first reading for another person indicates the involvement of both the glandular and the nervous systems in this particular disorder:

Now, as we find, there is rather complication of disturbances. Though these arise from specific disturbances or causes, the effect upon the physical forces are of a complex nature. These have to do primarily with the effect upon the glandular system. But the destructive forces affect more directly the nervous system, owing to the manner in which there is a defection in the coordination between the cerebrospinal and the sympathetic or vegetative nervous system in their reaction in the body.

Hence we have the effect of an agitans as it were, or a palsied condition affecting the locomotories more than the cerebrospinal or reflexes.

Hence the complication which arises in the disturbing forces of the body.   (1555-1)

Four months later, when this fellow applied for a second physical reading, he reported that the instructions given in the first had been followed and there was some improvement in his condition. This was confirmed at the outset of the second reading:

Now as we find, there are improvements in the general reactions in the bodily forces.

If there were greater consistency in the activities of the body, not only in the application of the electrical forces that have been given but used in the manner that has been outlined, it would make for a much better reaction.

Then, there must also be consistency in the manner of life—and its application of its abilities towards constructive forces or influences.

Is the body to be saved from physical disturbance that the real self or soul is to be purged into greater depths of disappointment and disdain?

Then let the physical and the mental and the spiritual coordinate, cooperate. Make the life more worthwhile, more purposeful. Arouse the activities of the mental and physical self to the better influence in a spiritual way and manner.

Not that the entity or body should become as one goody-goody, or sanctimonious or the like, but rather use consistency.

What is thy ideal? What is the outlook upon the experiences in the associations with others? Is it only for the gratifying of appetites, only for the self-indulgence for the moment? Can these do anything but weaken the physical as well as the better self?

Use then the manipulations and the vibrations of the low electrical forces, as indicated.

Then, if the body-mind is to be made more consistent with constructive forces in its dealings with not only itself but its fellow man, we will find the outlook upon life, the hopes and aspirations will be more in accord with that which is not merely ideal but constructive—and the life

and the associations will become more and more worthwhile.

Think on these things. Ye have abilities, ye have a promise. What are ye doing with thy soul?   (1555-2)

An excellent example of the holistic approach to healing,
which is a hallmark of the Edgar Cayce readings, is found in the
following case:

In considering that as may prove helpful for this body, it
will be well to consider the *entity* as a unit, if there would
be real help.

For, while we find there are pathological disturbances,
these in their very nature indicate a prenatal disposition.
Thus, if there would be physical or material help, the
body's first approach will necessarily be the study of self.

Not in that attitude, 'I didn't cause it,' and 'I wasn't the
effect of being brought into the earth,' neither in the
condeming of someone else for those attitudes or the lack
of consideration before the birth.

But rather consider that the self is being given an opportunity, here and now—if it will accept same—to interpret,
to understand, and to be of help not only to self but in contributing something to the welfare of others in all their
stages of development or seeking for physical, mental and
spiritual help.

That the prenatal condition existed is evidenced by the
cycle or period when these disturbances first appeared
with the body, in the lack of those elements or abilities
within the body-forces to reproduce the stamina necessary—in the nerves and muscles of the locomotory centers—for the use of same in a physically constructive,
creative way or manner.

That there was the so-called *meriting* of this interpretation, this understanding for this soul-entity, is indicated
by the soul's choice and use of this opportunity for en-

trance into material manifestation. Then, as you chose it, as you needed it, interpret it properly.

Do not become one that finds fault with others, condemns others. For, know—as given of old—'Though He were the Son, yet even He learned obedience through the things which He suffered.'

Would you be greater than the Son, who is the Way, the Truth and the Light? And through Whom you may have that promise fulfilled, that where two agree concerning anything and ask, they shall receive it—provided they live and be that which they ask?

Learn those lessons, then, knowing that as there were those elements lacking, there is the need for the proper interpretation in self along those lines!

Use those abilities of the mind in such measures and manners as to be ever a contributing influence for the creating of peace, harmony, love, kindness, gentleness, hope, in the minds and in the hearts of all with whom you come in contact day by day.

These are the first prerequisites if you would find help.

If you cannot accept this, forget it all. Do not even begin.

But do accept; that you may know the truth, that may indeed set you free—in body, in mind, in spirit; that you may indeed be one with Him.

Those elements of gold and silver were lacking in those periods of gestation, which produced in the first cycle of activity the inability of the glands to create.

At the present time these may be so administered to the body as to become a part of the building structural forces, being assimilated in such a manner as to contribute to the physical well-being of the body; though such—in many quarters—becomes questionable.   (3100-1)

There are changes, yet not all for good. While the system has been cleared and is from time to time changing in some respects for good, the progressive paralysis, or the paralysis agitans grows more progressive.

In these if the body will accept it there is the meeting of self—or karmic conditions.

Can it be healed? Yes, but the attitude of the body, the faith in the Divine, must not merely be assumed or proclaimed—it must be practiced in the daily life with others. This, added to that as may be had in the use of the Wet Cell Appliance which will carry these three elements into the body vibratorially, and then lived in activity not merely in words, but lived, may bring not only the staying of the condition, but like the elements which have been given stay the swelling, stay that activity of the disturbing forces.   (3468-3)

Several brief excerpts are included here which give definite hope for a cure. Emphasis is on a holistic approach in the suggested treatment. The patient, in each instance, is told to make application mentally and spiritually, as well as physically.

Can my condition be cured?
We're going to help it a lot!

Be prayerful in what you do. Use thy abilities of the strength that is given thee through the use of these elements suggested, that are to supply those forces lacking in body from the one source. Give the credit, the praise to Him, Who is the giver of all good and perfect gifts.   (3310-1)

Or, there is a wasting away of the nerve plexus from the centers of locomotion, in the cerebrospinal and sympathetic system; so that there is the lack of stamina in same.

This, as we find, may be materially aided if there is the *consistent* application of those things as we find that may add *to* the system in such a manner as to break down that which has been gradually builded, and gradually resuscitate broken cells.   (1618-1)

Either adhere to the suggestions given, *consistently,* or revert to the old positions or conditions. *Do not* attempt to mix same so much.

We would keep, then, those things as suggested, in the manners as indicated?

Either give this, then, the fair trial, *honest* trial, or *forget* it. (754-2)

Alcoholism

Today alcoholism is recognized as a disease. It frequently seems to be a karmic condition, which can be traced to overindulgence in one or more prior lives. In fact, based on the reading extract which follows, nicotine addiction may fall in the same category! Several individuals who apparently entered this earth-experience with a proclivity towards alcoholism, based on earlier excesses that may have contributed to their downfall in the past, were warned to avoid overindulgence and beware of strong drink or alcohol in any form.

Parents were sometimes warned to beware in this regard for their developing offspring. A reading given for an eight-year-old boy warned that the influence from a Roman life—involving excessive use of alcohol and nicotine—could become a stumbling-stone:

Beware, ever, of two influences in the life from that experience in this sojourn: nicotine in any form, and alcohol in its hard forms. These will become stumbling experiences if there are indulgences in those directions such that they become habitual in the inclinations of the influences that arise not only as appetites but as the emotions, or sensory forces of the body; for these will be easily influenced by such. (1417-1)

This man had emotional problems or attitudes which came from a still earlier life than his Roman sojourn: they were traceable to Atlantis. His excessive indulgence in strong drinks, during his Roman days, may have been a subconscious means of evading, or literally "drowning out," karma "brought over" from Atlantean times. Now he must face that earlier karma, as well as guard against what we might term the "psychological karma" of alcoholism from his Roman period. As the readings often stress, God is not mocked; and what has been sown must be reaped. Ultimately we are called upon to meet ourselves.

Another warning against strong drink was given in a reading for a 14-year-old girl. Not only did the reading caution her parents, it warned the young lady herself of future associations and appetites that could bode ill. "Here we find very unusual abilities," the reading stated in part, "and also some very unusual warnings to be given for such a lovely person." More of the reading follows:

> There will be these as warnings, these for those responsible for the entity: A tendency for the body to over-eat or to be overindulgent in appetites. Be warned for self, as well as associates of those who take wine or strong drink, for this may easily become a stumbling block to the entity.
>
> Before this we find the entity was in the land during those reconstructions following the period called the American Revolution. Here we find the entity interested in building a home with the beautiful grounds about same.
>
> In the name then Lila Chapman, the entity gained through the period, for the home to the entity and its family, and its children was that which took the greater portion of its time save the study of the Word which was given place in that home; and yet there came from same those who took too much of the cup as cheers. This brought disturbances, sorrows. Don't let it occur again. There will be the tendencies for attraction, not only for self, but for those about you. For that ye hate has come upon thee.
>
> Don't hate anything in the present.   (5359-1)

Is it not fascinating to note that we can as readily fall victim to those things we have hated, and condemned in others, as trip on those things in which we have overindulged ourselves in the past? Both extremes can be stumbling blocks!

A report from the mother confirmed this girl's tendency for overindulgence in food. Moreover, the reading was truly prophetic as to associations. She married several years later into what her mother called a "drinky" family, although her husband was apparently quite sensible and moderate in his drinking habits, which was fortunate.

In the next case, the person appears to have become an alcoholic due to his mental attitudes:

As we find, while there are physical disturbances with this body, these arise as much from the mental attitudes—that were in the beginning taken as poses, and have grown to become rather conditions that are of the *self;* or as habits, as requirements, that have taken on those aspects from the *mental* standpoint that are almost—or at times, and under or in certain environments, become—*possessions!*

For in its final analysis, in the physical and mental activities of a body, it—the body—*mentally*—is continually meeting itself and that it (the body, mentally) has done about *constructive* or creative forces within the body itself.

Then, as we find, to meet the needs of the conditions in this body, it must—or will—require that which will enable the body to either *become* determined within itself to *meet* its own self in *spiritual* reaction, or such a change of environment that will require the mental and physical reactions of the body to be such as to *enable* it (the body, mentally and physically) to *induce* that within the physical reactions to take possession in the place of, or to replace, those habit-forming conditions in the mental, as to rid the body of these conditions. (1106-1)

A second reading gave further insight as to how the appetite develops, weakening the will to point where one is virtually possessed.

Now, as we find, all the circumstances and conditions that disturb the body—both from the physical and mental angle—should be taken into consideration; if there will be in the experience the help, the aid that is desirable.

We find that the appetites—or the habits *and* appetites that have been created by the activities of the body—are of the nature of *both* the physical and mental attitudes towards conditions and circumstances.

Through resentments from little things that have been said, the body has allowed itself to build that appetite which in destroying the will of the entity—through the activities of drink upon the system—has produced a weakness that will require a great deal of mental determination; that must be based upon the spiritual self from within. And there must be the application also of material things which will aid in creating a balance to the assimilating system—the liver, the spleen, the pancreas, the kidneys; so that the great desires from associations do not again *overcome* the will-influence of the body.

These necessarily must be choices, or there must be a choice made by the mental body itself. First, that it would of its own accord submit to the treatments under such directions as may be had in the institution—such a one as in Nashville—for inebriates.

And with the submitting to the treatments, the applications, the weights, the tests—if the body will then keep away from the associations that have caused much of the activities, and engage itself mentally and physically *in* those activities that are the more constructive in their natures—then we may find not only material employment but an activity in the mental and physical life that will bring contentment and peace and harmony, and a life of

130.

useful service to others. And with prayer—determining in self, the aid and cooperation of those near and dear to the body in the mental and material ways—we may bring the better conditions for this body.

Is a cure within myself or is the treatment in an institution necessary?

To be sure, unless there is the determination within self to rid self of the appetites and desires builded in the will forces of the system, that have been to such extent as to produce physical reactions, then the cure may not be accomplished even in an institution—without the will in self of this to be so. But as we find, as we have indicated, the institutional treatments are necessary—with the determination within self.

And it will be easier, more desirable for the body to go through the institutional treatments.

Do that, then: relying upon those things that have been pointed out: that the basis of all spiritual awakening, the promises of the better and closer association with the Divine are within self.   (1106-2)

Another case gives further understanding as to how an appetite can develop to one's undoing. This reading says that physical disturbances which "appear to be minor, are deep-seated and come from pressures between the coordinating of the sensory forces and the activities of the deeper organs." It continues:

Thus we have periods when there are greater disturbances that find their reaction in gratifying of appetites.

Thus we have the effect of that the body would do in reasoning becomes that the body does not really *desire* to do in the physical, but the pressures are of such a nature that we have not a mental aberration or a mental disturbance, though the effects are in the physical that same character of reaction.

131.

Thus we have the conditions such that there becomes the gratifying of appetites in the bodily system, or desires.

And we find the body then, rather than as planning for that which is destructive in the mental abilities and mental attitude of the body, becomes so overwrought by physical desires as to necessitate the gratifying of physical appetites.

Not a possession, save when there begins the gratifying of same; *then* there are the opportunities for those influences from without to possess the activities of the body in not only the cunningness of the activities but in that which to the *body* under the influence, becomes as reasonableness to the influences and activities of that possession.

Have my former activities been such as to make for development as looked on from the soul forces?

These have been rather a tendency toward retardments in some directions, developments in others.

The *body* physically or soully, is not held for that which has become as appetites. Then to *condemn* self, in the activity toward others, is to *build* that which is destructive.

But with the attuning of the body physically and mentally, and *constructive* thoughts, putting that *behind* that has made for those influences wherein the body became easily influenced, we will find constructive forces becoming more and more predominant in the physical activities.

Is there any hereditary influence that has caused this moral letdown?

This is rather as that of possession through weaknesses created by appetites and physical conditions in the body.

(1439-1)

It isn't the intention, it isn't the inclination of the body to give way to such influences! It is rather the *increasing* of the appetites by the directions of same through the physical body! (1439-2)

In reading 606-1, it becomes apparent that no general outline of treatment can be given for alcoholic cases. And the same, presumably, would be true regarding any other disease. As explained by Cayce, "Each individual has its own individual problems."

Now, to build that resistance required to bring normalcy for this body: and *we* find that this may build this resistance in the nerve forces, that will aid in the nerve impulses in the ganglia that are so disordered here, as to reproduce nerve ends in the system and the *repulsion* by the strengthening of these will bring normalcy for this body.

Gold chloride and bromide of soda were recommended. Alcohol won't work with gold! This is the gold treatment, but it builds the resistance!

Massage and massage activity will be helpful; as well as keeping in the open all the time.

Do this, and we will bring normalcy for this body.

In alcoholic cases, can a general outline of treatment be given?

No. Each individual has its own individual problems. Not all are *physical*. Hence there are those that are of the sympathetic nature, or where there has been the possession by the very activity of same; but gold will destroy desire in any of them! (606-1)

Some people may wonder how gold works to quell a physical appetite, or desire, but gold is a symbol of the highest spiritual qualities.

The treatments Cayce recommended for overcoming alcoholism varied from physical therapy to inducing nausea and even to the use of electrical treatments—although a cautionary word was given that electricity and alcohol, together, would produce an *adverse* effect! The readings suggest that to be effective, the treatment must be tailored to the individual's attitudes and responses: he had to *want* to overcome the habit, first of all

133.

and must exert his willpower, which had been weakened by alcohol, to meet the situation. The strengthening effect of prayer could be vital in this regard, it was indicated.

One individual, who had a number of readings from Cayce, was apparently tempted to overindulge in alcohol. In one reading, he asked: "What general rules and precautions should I take to keep in a healthy condition?"

The answer:

As has been indicated. Do not *drink*, but *eat properly!* Do not *abuse* the body—either mentally *or* physically, but *most* of all by alcohol; and especially hops or the products of same, or even the carbonated waters are harmful for *this* body—and, of course, the *strong* drinks are more harmful!

For, too much of anything as of hops or alcohol reaction with same—with the very nature of the disturbance—produces in the liver, in the kidneys, the disturbances that *destroy* the effect of that plasm in the blood which aids in the eliminations of used energies; and produces toxic forces in the body. (391-18)

Prayer, and the desire to do right (already inherent in the character of this particular individual), were given as the way of escape from alcoholism in the following case:

Can those assisting do anything to prevent the body from indulging in stimulants?

They can pray like the devil!

And this is not a blasphemous statement, as it may appear—to some. For, if there is any busier body, with those influences that have to do with the spirit of indulgence of any nature, than that ye call satan or the devil, who is it?

Then it behooves those who have the interest of such a body at heart to not only pray for him but *with* him; and in just as earnest, just as sincere, just as continuous a manner as the spirit of *any* indulgence works upon those who have become subject to such influences either through physical, mental or material conditions!

For the *power* of prayer is *not* met even by satan or the devil himself.

Hence with that attitude of being as persistent as the desire for indulgence, or as persistent as the devil, ye will find ye will bring a strength. But if ye do so doubting, ye are already half lost.

For the *desires* of the body are to do *right!* Then aid those desires in the right direction; for the power of right *exceeds*—ever and always.

Do that, then.

Like the devil himself—*pray!*

Is it believed that there is any inclination in the body here to cooperate and correct these conditions?

As just given, it is *not* the real *desire* of the body to commit self to the inclination. There *is* the desire, then, to cooperate.

Hence there has been given the way to overcome— through the *physical* manner, the *mental* manner; and the *attitudes*.

Then let the body cooperate by putting behind self those things that easily beset. And look—*look*—to the strength and the power of the Christ-Consciousness—the light *within*; and be able to say *NO!* and mean it.   (1439-2)

Finally, here is another case where prayer was recommended:

And if the mental and spiritual forces are acted upon by those that have an interest in the welfare of the mental and spiritual reactions of this body, through the power of intercession by meditation and prayer, to counteract the forces from without that are working with this body, there may be brought an awakening within—in correcting these conditions—and awareness that there is a worthwhile experience for self in the activities of the entity's manifestation of life, and will bring the abilities to be active in directions that would make for a change that will not only be helpful, hopeful, but worthwhile.

Who may make the intercession? They that have within their consciousness a channel to the Throne of Grace, that there may be given into the mind and activities of the soul of this entity those influences that may bring the changes in the experience of this body.

In what manner may his sister help him?

By making the stronger intercession in prayer, and in getting or asking others to aid in and with her in same. For, where there is that intercession made through the combined efforts of many, the greater may be that directed influence towards the activity of any soul, any mental being.   (496-1)

Homosexuality

A much-discussed and controversial physical condition is homosexuality, which the Edgar Cayce readings indicate to be mainly karmic in its origins. The readings throw a great deal of fresh light on this subject, which tends to contradict the popular view of many psychologists that homosexual traits are primarily the result of a home environment in which the child is caught in an emotional crossfire between a dominant and overprotective mother and a weak father, or similarly unnatural "triangles" or relationships that distort the natural sexual inclinations of the developing adolescent.

It is not all that simplistic, if we may judge by the readings. And while one is led to the conclusion that homosexuality is not to be regarded by society as a *natural* life-style, inasmuch as the readings make it amply clear that the sexual function is for *procreation* rather than self-indulgence, neither should we condemn the homosexual or seek to restrict or limit his civil rights.

As a matter of fact, it was revealed in some of the readings for those who came to Mr. Cayce for help in meeting latent or manifest homosexual tendencies that they had mocked others with these very traits, in a prior life, and were now meeting similar urges within themselves! In other cases, homosexual tendencies could be traced to an earlier life in the opposite sex (most probably just prior to the present experience), and a difficulty in making the transition.

The readings generally encouraged those with homosexual tendencies to work towards a *normal* sexual development, rather than foster and promote their homosexual inclinations through a form of sexual gratification that would apparently hinder soul development. Even where the urges of a homosexual nature could not be totally overcome, it was intimated that the entity could use its affliction (for thus it seemed to be regarded) as a stepping stone, rather than a stumbling block: its creative energies could presumably be diverted to other uses—such as a musical career, in one instance—while at the same time, there would undoubtedly be a closer-than-normal rapport with members of the same sex, which could result in warm and rewarding friendships that could contribute much to the soul development of the entity and those affected by him.

These are the conclusions one inevitably draws from a careful study of the Edgar Cayce readings on this sensitive social issue that confronts us much more openly today than several decades ago, when the readings were given. At that time, the individuals approaching Mr. Cayce were usually loathe to make an open declaration to him of their problem, and there was no attempt in the readings to make embarrassing disclosures.

Thus, one often has to "read between the lines" in reaching a proper interpretation of the information given. But it is there; and it *can* be interpreted aright, particularly if one is familiar with the Cayce philosophy on such related subjects as sex, home, marriage, and so forth.

Here, for example, in a reading dealing with the question of sex and sex relations "as related to delinquency of the teens and younger ages," we find some pertinent observations:

This is ever, and will ever be, a question, a problem, until there is the greater spiritual awakening within man's experience that this phase biologically, sociologically, or even from the analogical experience, must be as a stepping-stone for the greater awakening; and as the exercising of an influence in man's experience in the Creative Forces for the reproduction of species, rather than for the satisfying or gratifying of a biological urge within the individual that partakes or has partaken of the first causes of man's encasement in body in the earth.

Are there any sex practices that should be abolished?

There are many sex *practices* in the various portions of this land, as in other lands, that should be—*must* be abolished. *How?* Only through the education of the *young!* The urge is inborn, to be sure; but if the purpose of those who bring individuals into being is only for expressing the beauty and love of the Creative Forces or God, the urge is different with such individuals. Why? It's the law; it's the LAW!

(5747-3)

A self-avowed homosexual was told that his problem went back ages ago to pre-Atlantean times, even before Adam!

The entity was among those who were then 'thought projections,' and the physical being had the union of sex in the one body, and yet a real musician on pipes or reed instruments.

Then, as indicated, we have those unusual experiences in the earth by the entity and the definite urges which are at variance to the general activities in the sex relationships. For in the experience in the Atlantean land, the entity sought to be both and wasn't very successful at either.

(5056-1)

138.

Apparently this confusion has been present throughout this person's earth lives, and it is a problem he was to work on in this life. He was given suggestions as to how to overcome this tendency. This involved strict self-discipline, including diet and work, and sleeping on a hard bed. He was also to work on his spiritual awakening, which would take him out of the troubling realm of physical feelings, so that mental and spiritual development could take place.

As to his abilities, he was told:

> There is nothing impossible for the entity to attain in fame or fortune, or in its spiritual unfoldment, and yet these will *not* be easy until the entity has conquered self.
>
> (5056-1)

A follow-up report, dated 1972, tells us that the young man did not work at correcting his physical condition, for he did not accept it as abnormal. Presumably he did not work on his "spiritual unfoldment" either, in the manner Cayce had outlined. And while he has become a musician of considerable merit, he has not attained the heights he was told he could achieve.

Another man was told that his homosexuality in the present came from a life in France during the period of Louis XIII and his successor, Louis XIV. Initially the entity was a writer, and the writings "made for political influences," he was told.

> Then there became the first of its artistic development in cartooning, and in the abilities to depict by placard or by the drawings those things or activities as to the political forces, as well as in the varied activities.
>
> Hence we find from those experiences a conflicting influence in the present; as the interest in art, interest in writing.
>
> Also the interests that arise from the associations or the relationships or experiences regarding sex come from

those conditions that were attempted to be depicted by the entity in its drawings, in its cartooning, in its making for an elaboration upon same.

There still (the cartoonings, drawings) may be found in the archives that have preserved much of that which dealt especially with Louis XIV and XIII.

In the application of that experience in the present, know that thou gainest little in the condemning of that in thine fellow man of which ye were *inwardly* guilty.

Condemn not, then, that ye be not condemned. For indeed with what measure ye mete it will be measured to thee again. And that thou condemnest in another (yea, every man—every woman), that thou becomest in thine self! (1089-3)

It is evident that the young man was experiencing some sort of retributive justice in the present. He had apparently caused others embarrassment and suffering from his satiric cartoons, so now he was experiencing like emotions. A later reading added this comment:

That there may be his unnatural affections, unnatural associations or relations, or desires, is as much *mental* as a physical condition! (1089-6)

In a different case, the person seeking help did not disclose the nature of his problem. The reading, however, immediately pinpointed the difficulty:

In analyzing the disturbances with this body, here we find not only the pathological conditions to be considered but the psychological. For, these are the effects of karmic influences, thus having to do with something being met in self in the present experience.

Here, the complete analysis of an entity's being might be proof of those tenets (to those who would study such) that

140.

life is a continuous experience. And where one has met self in those activities having to do with the psychological (that is, the soul-self), as in this body, and also the physiological—or the physical body and its relationships to the spiritual or psychic body, as in this condition here—there is brought a homosexual disturbance that is to the body a mental and a physical condition to be met.

These, then, are the conditions to be met.

For, with the relationships in mind, in body of such, as to open the cells in the Leydigian (leyden) forces, there is the flow of the kundalini in and through the body which finds expression in the organs of the sensory system; not merely to the disgust but to the shame of the body in itself—and yet these become a part of the whole body-mind and being.

Thus there is brought not merely a physical or purely pathological condition, but a physiological and psychological disturbance to the body.

These, as we find, can be met, by the mind and by that which is a part of the electrical forces of the body itself. Thus these, as we find, will be the applications. If these are used we may correct these disturbances, in self, in mind, in body, in the physical reactions.   (3364-1)

The young man was directed to use Atomidine (an iodine-based solution, which the readings often mentioned in connection with purifying the endocrine glands) and the Wet Cell Appliance. Also:

Live and keep normal activities. Begin with the study of self—not anatomically but spiritually. And the greater spiritual lesson you may gain is in the 5th chapter of Matthew. Learn this by heart, then read the 14th chapter of John and the 12th chapter of Romans.

Then live them!

Live them in thy daily relationships to others. Know

141.

that these words are spoken to thee. Apply these with thy application of the mechanical and material things of the body. (3364-1)

As we see, Cayce was applying holistic healing concepts to homosexuality, as he did to other disorders or bodily disturbances!

Another case:

In analyzing the records here, we find that while there are turmoils and strifes within self, these may be best met if the entity seeks to find its relationships first to the Creative Forces as indicated by Paul in his message to the Romans. Don't think more highly of yourself than you ought to, but if you don't think well of yourself, who will? But know that the power within is not of yourself but the grace of God. Your ability or your consciousness in the present is lent thee as an opportunity—because He hath first loved thee, as ye should love Him.

Then ye may be sure that as the purpose and desire is set in motion the material expression will be in keeping with that which will ever be creative in thy experience, and in those fields of service where ye may contribute to the welfare of the physical and mental well-being. For when man has learned that the physician must be the physician to the soul as well as to the body, he will have begun to find the meaning that the Great Physician gave to His ministry in the earth. As He indicated, which is it easier to say, 'Son, thy sins be forgiven thee,' or 'Rise, take up thy bed and walk'? [Matthew 9:5.]

Learn the meaning of such.

What is the reason for my sexual deviation and how should I face this problem?

By the application of the same things that we are giving that ye shall apply to others—hydrotherapy and electrotherapy. (3545-1)

The reading was given for this young man, in 1943 when he was 23 years of age. At the time, he was considering a career in hydrotherapy, which accounts for the answer given to his question. He later married and had one son. Whether he wholly overcame his homosexual tendencies is not known, but it would seem that he did.

Physiological Characteristics and Defects

Our bodily shape or structure is really part of our karma, according to the Edgar Cayce readings. Thus, a girl of 17 was told that her obesity, though physically a glandular condition, was also karmic. Her condition came from a life during Grecian and Roman times when she was an athlete:

Before that (among those making for the influence; and that becomes a great part of the general inclinations— physical—and creative mentally from the inner or intuitive activity) we find the entity was in the Roman and Grecian land, when there was the exchange of the games that were as part of what is now known as international or national athletic activity.

There we find the entity excelled in beauty, in the ability to carry in figure, in body, the games that were a part of the experience.

And too oft did the entity laugh at those less nimble of activity, owing to their heaviness in body.

Hence we find the entity not only meeting same in the present from a physical angle but there are the *necessities* of it being worked out by a diet as *well* as outdoor activity.

Thus we find that in the present from that experience, grace and beauty and the need for precautions become a part of what may be called—or are called by some—karmic forces.

Hence the *necessity* for the entity often taking self in hand and applying will in those directions that will make for growth in mental, material, and spiritual development.

For the necessity of such is a part of the experience of all, yet in the present experience for the entity—this entity—to enjoy the more of the material blessings as well as the personal satisfaction in being equal to others—it is necessary to take self in hand in those directions.

The name then was Amededoen; and from that experience there is still much in the way of those things that were—as would be termed in the present—as tokens of the abilities of the entity, that have an influence in the present.

(1339-1)

A woman of forty-five learned that her eventual blindness in one eye could be traced to her abuse of "the power of the eye" in an early Persian incarnation:

In the...land of the nomads or in the outer edge of now Arabian deserts, and the entity then the follower in that of the Bedouins, and given as the most beautiful of that group to which the entity belonged. The name then in that of Inxa, and the entity then ruled many through the power of the eye over the condition created in the minds of those whom this would subjugate to her way of reason. In the personality as exhibited today, we find in the patience and persistence in the condition, thought or felt to be aright, still able to control many through the eye and expression of same.

(538-9)

But fourteen years later, she developed iritis and became totally blind in one eye.

Is there any chance of restoring any part of the vision of the right eye?

Do all that may be possible. This will depend upon many general conditions, you see.

(538-65)

Treatment was given, which helped nominally. Vision,

however, was not restored. By a quite interesting coincidence, another case of eye trouble—congenital cataracts—was also traceable to the same early Persian period, although the karmic implications were quite different. This particular entity, it seems, was "given to what would be termed activities of a barbaric nature" in that experience, blinding captives from other tribes with hot irons!

There we find the entity came as a dweller from among the Persian peoples; given to what would be termed activities of a barbaric nature in its early experience. For the entity brought persecution to those of other tribes or other beliefs, by blinding with hot irons.

Such activities the entity forsook in those experiences when there was the awareness of the activities of the teacher in the 'city of the hills'—that teacher who gave those interpretations to the peoples as pertaining to that as would bring greater hope to those disappointed or discouraged, either in body or in mind.

And the entity became the leader in the musical instruments that were a part of the healing through those periods.

Hence, as indicated, those fields of activity in the present in which the entity may be the musician—especially of stringed instruments, or an individual applying the higher vibrations in electrical applications for healing, or the combinations of these—would be the fields of service in which the entity may find greater contentment, and an outlet for the emotions, the longings within, as may be experienced by the entity in the present sojourn.   (1861-2)

Here, again, the aptness of the condition seems to point to some sort of retributive justice. And, once more, we have music with its high vibrations recommended as an aid to healing. This man had blinded others, but eventually abandoned that cruel practice to aid in healing through music; thus both good and bad karma pursued him in this life, and he found himself on the verge of blindness but able to find the "greater contentment" and "outlet for the emotions" in "applying the higher vibrations in electrical applications for healing."

As the Edgar Cayce readings so often state, we are ever meeting ourselves; and what we have sown must be reaped eventually.

Nevertheless, by following the directions given in his readings, this man did regain partial vision. He also became an accomplished musician and music teacher.

Color blindness, which is apparently hereditary, was also karmic in a case with origins in a life in Atlantis. The man was told that this condition could be corrected:

Before that we find the entity was in the Atlantean land, during those periods when there began to be the rebellious forces that disputed those acts and laws pertaining to the communications with what is termed in the present as the unseen forces—or to those hierarchies that are given rule over activities in the various forms in the earth.

The entity then, in the name Al-Aar, was the ruler of those forces of the Law of One; and those activities that were raised against the entity's activities by the Beelzebubs make for an influence in the *physical* forces of the body of the entity in the present. Not that which may not be arighted, if the entity—as then—be not turned aside; irrespective of what may attempt to divert or to alter the purposes from the whole manifestation of the spirit of truth and light and love. Once lost in this direction, again those greater shadows of those impending forces that the entity saw in those mighty upheavals from the destructive forces used for the people from the prisms' activities and from the fires that were started for the fires of the deeper inferno that brought to the surface those destructive forces as from nature's storehouse itself. Yet the entity may, applying those same tenets that were held to in that period, make for the greater or farther advancement in the present. Much might and power are in thine inner self, my son. Keep those inviolate, if ye would be directed in that whereunto thou may indeed explore those fields of service and activity that may bring not only pleasure, comfort and ease but—most of all—to thy fellow man the greater knowledge of the love of the Divine that would free each soul, if it will but acknowledge His presence as the motivative influence in all its associations and dealings with its fellow man. Not for self, but less and less of self, and more and more for the glory of Him that came to His own, and His own received Him not. But as thou hast heard Him, even as Al-Aar, as thou directed those in bringing for thy fellows in the varied lands the knowledge of the Law of One, so may thou in thine activities in the present rise not only to the greater cause of satisfying those innate longings, but may rise to the power not for self, but for thy fellow man—such as to bring to thee thine greater development, thine own illumination and thine own understanding. And in all thy getting, get love—with the deep understanding.

Should I take an active interest in aviation?

This is a portion of thyself, and would be a portion of the new association and relations indirectly.

Would color blindness prevent my success?

The correction here, as indicated, may be made that will overcome this.   (820-1)

Is it not extraordinary that this man was told that he knew the Christ *during this lifetime in Atlantis?* Perhaps the impact and scope of karma is far greater than we have ever dreamed.

Another man was told in his reading that a foot problem in the present came from a former life, which was during the Gold Rush of 1849. We have practically no details as to the specific foot ailment, although he apparently was suffering from a chronic condition.

In the one before this we find in that period known as the Gold Rush, in the forty-nine's then the entity among those who journeyed westward, being then of that name Hambeing. The entity lost in the experience, only gaining of this world's goods much. Not taking *from*, directly—but running over *many* to attain same, and in that land may there yet be seen piles of stone set up by Sol Hambeing in that land. In the experience, the entity finds in the present, that 'No man may ever say that a wrong, *intentionally*, has been done him by me.' In *this* the entity suffered much physically, and in the experience the feet has brought much in of that suffered in *that* experience.   (99-6)

Whereas this man's westward trudge to gain a personal fortune for himself in the Gold Rush of '49 brought a karmic carryover of painful feet in his present existence, we find an interesting contrast in this next case.

A woman seems to have merited at least one aspect of good karma from a former life of drudgery, for the reading indicated that she had shapely feet in the present:

For the entity was then a teacher, school teacher. Drudgery was part of the experience and this innately gives manifestation to the entity in the dread of drudgery. But know, those who would do good must pay the price and there is much more to be had in the satisfaction of contributing something to the welfare of many than being the drudge servant of one who would mistreat even the better urges of the entity. Thus study well before there are considerations of joining another, for these activities are those wherein you had troubles before and eventually brought most of that you considered drudgery; while music, song, brought the only means of giving full expression (hasn't the body got a beautiful foot?) in the activities which brought the greater expression, greater experience for the entity in the name of Lila Cox.   (5365-1)

A question in a later questionnaire on her reading asked: "Do you have, according to your own and others' estimation, 'a beautiful foot'?" Her answer: "I suppose. It is smaller than most girls of my height."

In reading 1286-1, we have another example of drudgery which brought reward in the next life. In her present life this woman became a model because of her unusually graceful hands. Her hands were so exceptionally beautiful that she was in demand to model jewelry and cosmetics such as hand lotion and nail polish. This enabled her to earn a good living from the many photographs of her hands, which were used in advertisements.

Before this, then, we find the entity was in the English land, during those periods when there was a great change in the religious activities of the peoples during the period of the studies of some of the religious forces that followed after those periods of the gatherings of groups for the defense, or in the Holy Wars.

The entity then took upon itself, with those of the younger forces or younger peoples, to become what is termed in the present a recluse—for the very activities in doing penance. And with the hands the greater labors were wrought.

Thus as may be seen in the experiences of the present, while those activities that made for oft the toil, the trial, the unsightly work of the hands even from the material angle of same, that which is as the promise to each and every soul in its expression; that whereunto there has been the expression of duty, love, patience, long-suffering, or an activity in a way and manner as to bring about in the experience of the soul-body the promises of the fruit of the spirit, may be brought and seen in the experiences the beauty in the hands, in the activities of same in the present.

The name then was Helaine Resnau, and there may be

seen even yet, in some of the abbeys of the English land the activities and preservations and influences of the Sister Helaine Resnau in those experiences.

In the application of self in these in the present, know— as was experienced then—the greater influence that may be brought to bear upon the associations and activities is in rather what the entity does about same; and how, in what manner one uses or applies self—and the prompting force that *impels* same! For what, first, is thy ideal? Is it in the spiritual, in the mental, in the material? For He, that is the Giver of all good and perfect gifts, may bring in thy experiences the glories, the beauties, the understandings of a purified, a glorified body, in the service of Him that is the Giver. (1286-1)

A beautiful, strong, healthy body may also present physical karma, which may or may not be on the "plus" side, depending upon the ideals and purposes of the individual who has presumably sought this type of physical expression. (Judas Iscariot, according to reading 5749-1, was "the better looking of the twelve"!)

At any rate, a Cayce reading told a man that his athletic prowess and strong body came from an Arabian life, where he taught and emphasized care of the physical body:

In the one then before this, we find in that land now known as the Arabian land, and during that period when there was being builded [a city] in the land about the caves that are now known as the town of Shuster. The entity then came as an emissary from what is now known as the Grecian land, coming as one that would bring to these peoples that of the care of the *physical* body, being sought by those [helpers] of the leader as a teacher for those that *would* know control of the physical body. In this experience the entity gained and lost. Gained through the lessons as were taught by the leader Uhjltd, losing in the aggrandizing of selfish interests when the passing of the leader left confusion for the time. From this experience, as Philas, the entity gains those of the influences in the athletic forces, or tendencies of physical prowess, of physical abilities in the various sports, games, of either those for defense or offence, or for sports—these have the appeal to the entity, yet are easily set aside for the more pressing matters of the hour.   (279-4)

Scars

Physical scars, as well as the scars of the soul, may be karmic. Reading 1165-1 explains that our physical expression, or body, as well as our personality and soul development, tend to reflect our past life experiences.

Yes, we have the body, and those conditions that surround the body. It is with its mother.

Now, in reference especially to those conditions that are indicated by the mark on the forehead and the cheek or side of head:

This might be expressed or manifested in many a way, or much might be given as respecting same—as to the pathological effects, as to the influences that arise from the psychological effects and the psychopathic effects that had to do with those things which manifest in this way and manner.

Rather would we approach same from that which we have indicated through these sources heretofore, as to how each individual in its manifestations in the earth bears within its physical expression the marks of that which has been or may be termed as an expression of a development in the soul and spiritual forces.

This is being sought, however, more from the material experience or expression; and that is being sought that may remove are to be a portion of the experience of the body—if it is to carry on in this experience.

As conditions change, or when it has reached nine months—then we would give those changes; if there remains within the innate desire of those that seek in the present for the periods when there begins then the developing of the *individuality*, rather than the personality of this soul expressing and manifesting itself as [the present person].   (1165-1)

In the following paragraph, one person was told how to handle scars:

As for scars, rather let the scars be removed from the mental and spiritual self.   To undertake such through those activities of anyone altering these, we will have worse scars.   Let the scars be removed from your own mental and spiritual self.   Turn to those things of making application of the fruits of the spirit of truth; love, patience, gentleness, long-suffering, brotherly love, putting away those little tendencies of being 'catty' at times or being selfish or expressing jealousy and such.

(5092-1)

"Let the scars be removed from your own mental and spiritual self"! Is that not touching upon the very heart of all physical karma? And what could better summarize the message of this book? It is the scars of the soul that should concern us, not the scars of the body. If we try to alter or remove the latter, we are told, "we will have worse scars." Then, *any* type of physical karma had best be left alone, if we are only seeking a *physical* healing, lest a worse thing befall us! The Master Himself made that same point.   What is needed, obviously, is the *triune* or holistic approach recommended in the Edgar Cayce readings, which treats body, mind, and soul, in recognition of the fact that they are *one*. Fortunately it is an approach to healing that is gaining broader and broader acceptance today.

Our next chapters deal with this subject.

CHAPTER FOUR

MEETING KARMA

The next question one would naturally ask is: Can a deep-seated physical karma be reversed or healed?

Physical karma is here understood to include psychological and psychosomatic dis-eases for they are essentially *physical* in their manifestation. The human brain is in the physical body and receives its impulses from the various bodily systems, especially from the neurological system; so that a mental problem is properly classified as a type of physical karma.

It is true that the answers given to various individuals, in connection with the question we have just posed, often appear conflicting in the Edgar Cayce readings. Some are given much encouragement, while others are given none or little. Yet sudden remissions and permanent healings do occur. Why is one person healed and another not healed? Has the karma of the former been met or paid? Or has the inner conflict ended? Is the individual who received a healing now under the Law of Grace? Must an entity pay "every jot and tittle," or does "grace" start to operate at some point?

It would seem that the degree of healing received depends entirely upon the individual and his responses. How much does one wish to be healed? Will the sufferer make the necessary effort to change his ways? And will he be persistent and consistent in following the prescribed treatments, cooperating fully in the recommended therapy?

The readings make it clear that the problem, while manifesting in the physical, is really to be met mainly on the mental or spiritual level, where it has its origins. Is the sufferer ready to acknowledge this, and turn to the Divine within, seeking attunement (or at-one-ment) with the Creative Forces, or God?

> To be sure, as it has been indicated again and again, there is that within the physical forces of the body—if it is kept in a constructive way and manner—which may be revivified or rejuvenated and kept in a constructive way and manner. This requires, necessarily, the proper thinking, the proper living, the proper application of those influences in the experience of an *entity* in its associations with everything about a body.   (681-2)

The examples of physical karma given in this book illustrate how very complex the real cause of physical karma is. Since karma is something "carried over," having originated in a prior earth-life, its causal aspects in the present life may appear as a direct manifestation, such as a defect or physical weakness apparent at the time of birth, for instance, or may be of an indirect nature, where the unsuspected "trigger-mechanism"—a seeming accident, a period of prolonged stress or wrongful living—may ignite the flame of a dormant karma at almost any stage of an entity's life. And this matter of timing, certain cases seem to suggest, may often be conditional upon the specific nature of the karma and the type of lesson needed by the entity to bring about a spiritual awakening.

We are body, mind and soul. Edgar Cayce said that to understand physical karma, we must look more toward the spiritual than anywhere else, since that is where the solution always lies. Yet the problem may manifest on any of the three levels of personal existence—physical, emotional or mental—or it may manifest simultaneously on all three levels. This indicates the complexity of the treatment for karmic ills.

Actually, the problem of meeting our karma is twofold. We can discuss it in terms of how a health professional or counselor might help a patient or client come to terms with repeated patterns of karmic illness in his or her life—and in terms of how an individual interested in self-improvement and growth can learn to recognize, understand, and transform these patterns on his or her own. In each case, however, the actual transformation of these patterns depends on the willingness of the individual to come face to face with himself or herself, accept it, and then begin working immediately to improve it—to heal the scars of the soul.

There is no medicine which can be administered to heal these scars, nor any plastic surgery which can remove them. And so, the challenge to the health professional or counselor is to work with love and patience to help the patient or client see his or her own role in generating ill health—and what can be done to change the underlying pattern. It is not necessary to know actual details from earlier lives to be successful in this endeavor. In fact, such knowledge sometimes is a distraction, as the patient or client becomes absorbed in speculation about who he or she was—rather than in honestly facing the changes which must be made! Far more important is an intelligent ability to see the karmic kinds of patterns at work—and to begin working directly to change them. In other words, in dealing with a person suffering from arthritis, the health professional or counselor should examine the person's attitudes, habits, and lifestyle and see what traits suggest a karmic pattern at work—a difficulty in relaxing, a lack of generosity toward others and life, and rigid ideas and opinions. Then, in addition to traditional forms of medical treatment for the arthritis, these karmic patterns should also be treated.

The patterns for meeting karma on our own are much the same. If you have reason to think you are suffering from some kind of physical karma, three basic questions arise: What is the probable root-cause of my condition? How can I best meet it, so that the karmic pattern will be broken? Is the condition curable?

The first question is answered within self. "Study to *analyze self*," states reading 2438-1. If this is done conscientiously, you will be able to uncover those negative traits, whether in the area of attitudes and emotions that create problems in your relationships with self and others, or some other aspect of your character makeup. No one knows us better than we know ourselves. The difficulty lies in facing ourselves willingly and honestly, so that we can proceed to "right about face."

In answer to the second question, then, the karmic cycle can only be broken by mending our ways.

And is the condition curable? "There are in truth no *incurable* conditions," says another of the readings. But it continues:

That which exists is and was produced from a first cause, and may be met or counteracted, or changed, for the condition is the breaking of a law, and the healing forces will of necessity become the compliance with other laws that meet the needs of the condition.

The evasion of a law only puts conditions off, and must eventually be met. (3744-1)

The concept of holistic healing that is encountered again and again in the Edgar Cayce readings is exemplified in case 1661, pointing to the need for an awakening within the person's "inner self" to "the relationships of the activities of self—physical, mental and spiritual—to the whole":

While there are deficiencies and defections in the physical reactions of the body, all of the activities, the hopes,

156.

the desires, the purposes and aims *must* be taken into consideration—in giving or in determining the activities for the body in regaining to *any* extent the use of the faculties of the physical forces.

For each body, through its experience in the material plane, is meeting its own self. And there needs be those developments, those awarenesses, those consciousnesses of the relationships of the activities of self—physical, mental and spiritual—to the whole.

Hence we may give, then, those activities which have caused and do cause these disturbances, but we would not hinder, we would not make other than a concerted activity in the awareness and in the awakening the consciousness of the entity's inner self to its relationship to the Creative Forces as may manifest through the entity's own self, as in relationships to its guards or guides in the material association and experiences. (1661-1)

And another person was told:

We find that the greater help here may come from spiritual insight and the trust in the Divine within self to carry forward with the purpose and aims in this material sojourn. (3305-1)

Here is how one individual was advised to change karma into grace:

This, of course, makes for conditions which are to be met, for what one sows that must one reap. This is unchangeable law. Know that this law may be turned into the law of grace and mercy by the individual, through living and acting in their lives in relationships to others. (5233-1)

The material body perishes, but life is a continuous stream

157.

of experience for the soul-entity. And so, quite naturally, the major emphasis in the readings was always on the spiritual, or what was termed soul-development. To experience a permanent healing, the individual had to attune to the Divine within, and change his attitudes and emotions, his actions and his thoughts, until they were in harmony with his spiritual ideals and purposes.

One must, however, work simultaneously on the physical level to get the human body in the best possible condition, in coordination with mental and spiritual changes being brought about. Many different and unusual kinds of therapy were recommended in the Edgar Cayce readings at one time or another. Yet some sort of physical therapy and diet were normally part of the treatment. In degenerative diseases, as noted in the previous chapter, the Wet Cell Appliance or the Radio-active Appliance were ordinarily advised. These appliances work on the electrical impulses within the cells of the body, thus strengthening and purifying the bodily forces. They also aid in attuning the body to the Creative Forces, or God.

In respect to the application of these electrical appliances, the following excerpt is instructive; and it should help us to realize that this form of healing modality, working on the principle of "the vibrations from *low* electrical forces," might require considerable time and patience in producing the desired results:

> In the application of this, these are the effects produced upon the body:
> *Life* in its expression in a human body is of an electrical nature. The vibrations from *low* electrical forces, rather than the *high* vibrations...produce life-flowing effects. Or the vibration begins as a movement of one-two in its molecule of atomic effect about a cycle of activity through the body. (988-7)

Treating the physical body changes only the effects or

symptoms, of course, not the causes. The sufferer is thus made more comfortable and the symptoms are temporarily relieved. This is a useful adjunct to the mental and spiritual phases of the healing work.

It is natural for one to want, and even to expect, an instantaneous healing—a miracle. And the law of expectancy, in certain cases, may bring this to pass. But are we really ready for it? Can we sustain such a healing if we have not learned our lessons well enough? One does not "hold on" to an ailment, of course; but we have already noted that it is through patience that growth is acquired:

> Learn ye patience, if ye would have an understanding, if ye would gain harmony and grace in this experience! 'For in patience do ye possess your souls.' (1201-2)

Even Jesus did not heal everyone. And He said, 'Go, and sin no more.' This surely meant to live aright. For true healing to take place, the entity must be ready both mentally and spiritually. This can be a slow process with some. In chronic cases, perhaps all bodily systems must be rebuilt, requiring at least a seven-year cycle. And yet:

> Do not be disheartened because of apparent slowness, but be patient and persistent; knowing that the activity which is best for the full mental and spiritual development will be attained—if the attitude and desire are held as indicated. (1215-7)

Sometimes there are sudden remissions. Disease symptoms clear up and disappear voluntarily. We may wonder why. Probably the individual, whether at a conscious or unconscious level, has been meeting the problem posed by his physical karma. When a sufficient degree of harmony is achieved within, the dis-ease has no further base for its perpetuation. It is driven out of the body.

On the other hand, a person who feels that he has properly met and overcome the karmic aspects of a given condition may find the condition slow to respond. Why? The answer can probably be found in this excerpt from one of the "Prayer Group" readings of Edgar Cayce:

Oft is a thorn left in the flesh to tempt, yea, to keep one aright. When one acquires the development to meet, or when one raises self to meeting all that is open, then self is healed also.   (281-18)

As already noted, there are no incurable diseases; but there are "incurable" people. That is, there are some who will not put forth the necessary effort to change mentally or spiritually, or to keep up the physical treatments recommended. And there are others who intentionally deceive themselves, with mock vows to mend their ways if they are healed:

For the body renews itself, every atom, in seven years. How have ye lived for the last seven? And then the seven before? What would ye do with thy mind and thy body if they were wholly restored to normalcy in this experience? Would these be put to the use of gratifying thine own appetites as at first? Will these be used for the magnifying of the appreciation of the love to the Infinite? For who healeth all thy diseases?   (3684-1)

How well do you wish to be? How well are ye willing to cooperate, coordinate with the Divine influences which may work in and through thee...?   (4021-1)

In order to meet the conditions of physical karma, our attitudes should first be examined:

In making for corrections, there must be a change of attitude—towards self, those about self, and the conditions which the body physically and mentally has found and does find around self.

Resentments, animosities, petty jealousies and the like must be eliminated as much as practical and possible, *if* there will be the better physical force, the better mental and physical reactions.

This as we find may best be done by the body analyzing itself. Consider: What is thy ideal? What is thy purpose?

And when considering the ideal, know that this—spiritually, mentally, materially—must find its basis of activity in spirituality—this is, prompted by the desire to do something that is constructive in the very physical forces and physical relationships.

Do not consider so much what others should do for or to *you*, but what will you do for and towards others?

And realize that all of these must be constructive in their nature.   (1889-1)

The Edgar Cayce readings make it evident that we live in a "law and order" universe. Karma implies that one or more of the laws of life has been violated in the past, and is now being balanced.

That which is in the physical disturbing is, ever, the result of breaking a law; either pertaining to the physical, mental, or spiritual.   (3220-1)

For an individual entity, with all the attributes of body, soul and spirit, is subject to the laws thereof; and until individuals are in their thought, purpose and intent *the law*—that is constructive—they are subject to same.

Hence those injunctions...'when ye know the truth, the truth shall indeed set you free.' From what? That of *self!*

And when they, as the story of old, blame someone else, it is the continuous warring within themselves. For their selves, their consciousness, their soul knows! And continues to war for the constructive experience in the activities with the influences about each entity.   (1538-1)

Prayer does help us to change. But prayer must be translated into action. Real change comes from the application of new insights and understanding gained through our periods of earnest prayer and self-examination. Change precedes growth. We know it is much easier to pray for healing than to discipline ourselves or change ingrained habits or negative thoughts. We can always seek help from the creative forces through consecrated prayer and meditation.

The poet, Robert Browning, expressed it well:

PRAYER

Unanswered yet? Nay, do not say ungranted;
Perhaps your part is not yet wholly done.
The work began when your first prayer was uttered,
And God will finish what He has begun.
If you will keep the incense burning there,
His glory you shall see, sometime, somewhere.

CHAPTER FIVE

HEALING THE SCARS

Physical karma, however severe, is a condition which can be eradicated through prayer and fasting. Fasting, however, has another interpretation than abstaining from food:

Fasting—as is ordinarily termed—is as the Master gave: Laying aside thine own concept of *how* or *what* should be done at this period, and let the *Spirit* guide. Get the *truth* of fasting! The body, the man's bodily functioning, to be sure, *overdone* brings shame to self, as overindulgence in anything—but the *true* fasting is casting out of self that as 'I would have done,' [replacing with] 'but as *Thou*, O Lord, seest fit—use me as the channel, as the strength comes by the concerted and cooperative seeking of many to give Thy strength to a body!' (295-6)

Spiritual attunement is the key:

The closer the body will keep to those [Biblical] truths

and the dependence on the abilities latent in self through trust in spiritual things, the quicker will be the response in the physical body. For all healing, mental or material, is attuning each atom of the body, each reflex of the brain forces, to an awareness of the Divine that lies within each atom, each cell of the body. (3384-2)

The following excerpts give further counsel and help for attuning to the Divine within, which brings healing:

Raising then in the inner self that image of the Christ, love of the God-Consciousness, is making the body so cleansed as to bar against all powers that would in any manner hinder. Be thou *clean* in Him. (281-13)

Make His presence a conscious thing in thy conversation, in thy dealings with they fellow man. For where the heart is, there the activity is to bring into the influence of those whom you meet that consciousness of that which is near and dear to thee.

Then as ye make the life, the love, the awareness of the Christ Consciousness in the Father in thy daily life, more and more are ye able to give that which will bring into the experiences of others that same awareness. For thoughts are things, and Mind is the Builder. (281-39)

Then, putting away doubt and fear, let that mind be in thee which was in Jesus, the Christ, as He prayed, 'Father forgive them, for they know not what they do.' (281-45)

For He stands at the door of thy heart, of thy consciousness; and as He has given, 'Ask in my name, believing and it shall be done unto thee.' What greater promise, greater blessing may come to any soul than to know that He cares—yea, that He is mindful of thy petitions, of thy aches, thy pains, thy disappointments, thy sorrows, thy joys, thy exultations. Then, stand ye as true friends of Him who gave His life that *all* might have life and have it more abundantly. (281-40)

Faith is another aspect of healing that can help us erase the scars of the soul. In James 5:15, it is written: "And the prayer of faith shall save him that is sick, and the Lord shall raise him up; and if he have committed sins, it shall be forgiven him."

Forgiveness, however, is a two-way street. One obstacle to our healing, which means being forgiven in the sight of God, may be our unwillingness to forgive others. Do we hold a grudge against another? Against ourselves? Against life itself?

Forgive, if ye would be forgiven. (262-97)

Never pity self, nor censure self. (279-4)

And what is life? God manifested in the material plane. For it is still in Him that we live and move and have our being. Thus life as a material manifestation is the expression of that universal force or energy we call God. (3590-1)

Prayer and meditation are co-partners in healing. But whereas prayer is a form of supplication, addressed to a Superior Being, meditation is an opening of the gate, as it were, so that the Christ may enter and we meet on common ground! Meditation, in a definition found in reading 1861-19, "is listening to the Divine within."

Be *oft* in prayer, oft in meditation, *seeing* self gaining the proper nourishment, proper resuscitating forces from those elements being given to the system for its resuscitation. (2097-1)

Thus prayer and meditation can be used to heal the scars. Indeed, the practice of meditation is perhaps the most important discipline for anyone seeking to know himself, or to obtain conscious union with God. (They are the same; for God and man are one.) Meditation is a technique of conscious self-realization—the pathway to light and the Christ Consciousness.

The term "meditation" is often used loosely to mean pondering, or thinking things over, or a state of "knowingness"; it is sometimes used interchangeably with the word "prayer." Prayer and meditation, although not synonymous, are very closely related. We pray creatively and most effectively after meditation. Moreover, prayer is often needed to prepare us properly for the state of meditation. We have to be calm and quiet in order to meditate; so we may need to ask God's help or forgiveness in order to quiet our minds and bodies.

As Jesus said in Matthew 5:23-24: "Therefore if thou bring thy gift to the altar, and there rememberest that thy brother hath aught against thee; leave there the gift before the altar, and go thy way; first be reconciled to thy brother, and then come and offer thy gift." Jesus could well have been referring to meditation, for it is a method of offering up self and gaining awareness of God. The sacred altar may be equated with the Christ Consciousness. Edgar Cayce said that the Christ Consciousness can be described as that awareness within each soul, imprinted in pattern on the mind and waiting to be awakened by the will, of the soul's oneness with God.

Explaining meditation, one of the readings states:

It is not musing, not daydreaming; but as ye find your bodies made up of the physical, mental, and spiritual, it is attuning of the mental body and the physical body to its spiritual source. It is the attuning of thy physical and mental attributes seeking to know the relationships to the Maker. That is true meditation.   (281-41)

Here are futher references, which help to differentiate between meditation and prayer:

Ye must learn to meditate—just as ye have learned to walk, to talk, to do any of the physical attributes of thy mind as compared to the relationships with the facts, the attitudes, the conditions, the environs of thy daily surroundings.   (281-41)

Then set definite periods for prayer; set definite periods for meditation.   Know the difference between each. Prayer, in short, is appealing to the Divine within self, the Divine from without self, and meditation is keeping still in body, in mind, in heart, listening, listening to the voice of thy Maker.   (5368-1)

For prayer is supplication for direction, for understanding. Meditation is listening to the Divine within. (1861-19)

Meditation, then, is prayer, but is prayer from *within* the *inner* self, and partakes not only of the physical inner man but the soul that is aroused by the spirit of man from within.   (281-13)

The A.R.E. Prayer Group (which was formed as the result of a dream Edgar Cayce had in 1931) was given this explanation of the difference between prayer and meditation after they had been working for some time with both:

Prayer is the concerted effort of the physical consciousness to become attuned to the consciousness of the Creator, either collectively or individually.   *Meditation* is emptying self of all that hinders from the creative forces rising along the natural channels of the physical man to be disseminated through those centers and sources that create the activities of the physical, the mental, the spiritual man; properly done must make one *stronger* mentally, physically, for has it not been given He went in the strength of that meat received for many days? Was it not given by Him who has shown us the Way, 'I have had meat that ye know not of'? As we give out, so does the *whole* of man—physically and mentally—become depleted, yet in entering into the silence, entering into the silence of meditation, with a clean hand, a clean body, a clean mind, we may receive that strength and power that fits each individual, each soul, for a greater activity in this material world.

(281-13)

Obviously when Jesus said, "I have meat ye know not of," He was referring to the benefits or results of communing with God the Father, which we call meditation. It is therefore part of the Christian teaching but is little understood.

Meditation is a vital part of all mystical religions. It is a technique that is taught in the major Oriental religious philosophies, such as Buddhism and Hinduism. Also, it is evident that many of the great Christian saints and teachers, down through the centuries, practiced the art of meditation, either consciously or unconsciously.

Actually, no matter what approach is used or what name applied, meditation remains precisely that. It is a mental discipline that begins with deep concentration and evolves up to the contemplative state. In the process, the physical and mental bodies of the practitioner are quieted, and the spiritual self takes over. When the conscious mind is still and focused, higher areas of the unconscious or the superconscious are reached. We might say that meditation is a movement in consciousness. Because of this, meditation is actually the doorway to direct experience at the spiritual level.

The Purpose of Meditation

To transcend from the world—to expand consciousness until it takes in other realms—this has ever been one of man's greatest yearnings. It is more than a dream: it is a part of the soul's memory, tracing back to our ancient heritage as the unfallen Sons and Daughters of God.

The purpose of meditation, according to the Cayce readings, is to attune the finite mind to the Infinite Mind, or God. This should never be attempted for selfish motives, which would lead to the soul's undoing. We are here in the earth for soul development. And each incarnation should be viewed as another cycle in our upward evolution, back to the Source whence we came.

That which is so hard to be understood in the minds or the experiences of many is that the activities of a soul are for self-development, yet must be selfless in its activity for it, the soul, to develop.   (275-39)

It is just as necessary that there be food for the spiritual and mental man as for the physical man — and this applies to self.

Take time first to be holy. Don't let a day go by without meditation and prayer for some definite purpose, and not for self, but that self may be the channel of help to someone else. For in helping others is the greater way to help self.   (3624-1)

Remember there is no shortcut to a consciousness of the God-Force. It is part of your own consciousness, but it cannot be realized by the simple desire to do so. Too often there is a tendency to want it and expect it without applying spiritual truth through the medium of mental processes. This is the only way to reach the gate. There are no shortcuts in metaphysics, no matter what is said by those who see visions, interpret numbers, or read stars. These may find urges, but they do not rule the will. Life is learning within self. You don't profess it, you learn it.
                        (5392-1)

The art of meditation is invaluable to soul development, but we are told:

Don't be anxious about it. Let it be a necessity to thy better being, rather than giving or having the meditation for better being. You have the meditation because you desire to be attuned with Creative Forces. You don't have the meditation because it's a duty or because you want to feel better, but to attune self to the Infinite!   (1861-18)

Hence as ye meditate, as ye analyze thyself—it isn't that there is to be given of the means so much, as it is to assist and aid others that ye meet day by day to analyze themselves—that they keep away from hate, animosity, jealousies, fears; those things that produce disturbing forces in the lives of thy neighbor, of thy friend, of thy people. Admonish them as He of old, that they walk in the ways that are in keeping with those things in which the Creative Forces or God are active, or are taken into the activities of the relationships day by day.   (1315-10)

Techniques for Attuning
We are told we must learn to meditate. How, then, do we go about it? To begin, there must be a strong desire to master the techniques and reach the goal.

1. *The Ideal.* Cayce emphasized the need to attune first to a proper ideal:

We would begin first, with the formulating of policies and attitudes for the balancing of the life principles and purposes.   (3624-1)

First, find thy ideal; and this will be an ideal manner of meditation. Then enter into same with a clean purpose, a clean desire, to be used and not to demand.   (2428-1)

Cayce clarified what he meant by the "proper ideal" in response to the following question:

170.

What is the exact means or method by which I can consciously reach the divine power or psychic force that is within me and draw upon it for the knowledge, strength, power and direction to accomplish great deeds that will bring about desired ends?

This lies latent, of course, within self. First find deep within self that purpose, that ideal to which ye would attain. Make that ideal one with thy purpose in Him. Know that within thine own body, thine own temple, He—thy Lord, thy Master—has promised to meet thee. Then as ye turn within, meditate upon those promises from body-mind (which is the soul and the mental self, or the Father *and* the Son in activity), so that there arises that consciousness of the at-onement with Him. And there may come—yea, there will come—those directions: by that constant communion with Him. *Use* this, practice this in thy daily dealings even as the Master, who made Himself one *with* His brethren, that He might save the more.   (2533-1)

2. *Time and Place*. Consistency and persistence are necessary in learning to meditate. Cayce indicated that the early morning hours are the best time for meditation. Probably this is because there are fewer distractions in the early hours. Most people are still sleeping, so that there are not so many vibrations in the atmosphere to disturb or distract one. Therefore, it is easier to quiet the mind and body, reaching that inner state of silence—listening for the still, small voice within.

Daily meditation at some definite time and place is highly desirable, if not an outright necessity, for the beginner.

Though Edgar Cayce told several people 2:00 a.m. was the best time to meditate or pray, he also indicated that the "best" time was actually whenever the individual found it most suitable or convenient, from a personal standpoint. One person was told to meditate at sunrise; and many people prefer this time. It may be that an exact time each day is difficult for some beginners to achieve, since the conscious mind does rebel at being disciplined and tends to present the body with sundry desires and distractions at the appointed time for meditation. Nevertheless, the neophyte will make more rapid progress if a fixed time and place are established at the outset, and then held inviolate. The habit of daily meditation will thus be firmly planted within a set routine, and it will be found that the conscious mind soon drops its former resistance and learns to cooperate.

Several quotations from the readings are presented on this subject of selecting an appropriate time-frame for meditation and prayer. They should encourage the beginner to establish his own time and rhythm; also, they should enable him to see that no one can really tell another exactly when, or even how, to meditate: one can only point the way.

What is my best time for meditation?
As would be for all, two to three o'clock in the morning is the best time.
Any other suitable time?
Any time. For how has the injunction been? 'Constant in prayer.' This is rather then that the whole attitude be kept in that attitude ever of a thankfulness. And leave it with Him. (462-8)

What are the best hours for meditation?
The best hour for meditation is two o'clock in the morning. The better period would be that which will be set as a period in which the body and mind may be dedicated to that. Then keep your promise to self, and to your inner self, and to your Maker, or that to which ye dedicate thy body, mind and soul. (2982-3)

Why is 2 a.m. the best time to meditate?
For the body-mind, as we find (if it has slept), the activities—of the physical body as it were, in that vibration where it is between the physical, the mental, and spiritual

activities of the body. If it is kept awake, it isn't a good time to meditate, but sleep, and then arise, and purposefully—for in prayer, so in meditation, let it be purposefully, and then don't abuse it—use it. Life is the manifestation of God—of the Creative Forces. So in prayer and in meditation. Prayer—He knoweth what ye have need of, but it is that love, that hope within self, knowing, feeling the desire to approach, thankful, prayerful, and then listen for direction. (1861-19)

What is the best time of day for me to seek greater attunement with the Infinite?

It is the material experience of the entity that this is changeable. At some periods it may be in the quietness even of the night-time, and at others even when the hands are the busiest—or the mind—there comes the awareness of the activity in the direction of the mental being, to the studies of this lesson or this thought.

Hence, as He has given, be constant in prayer, be watchful, and be mindful of that which may be obtained when the self is in attune, when there is felt, seen, heard the expressions of that which may come over, in, or through the mental being. (262-56)

This last paragraph definitely tells us that guidance will come when one is attuned, the impressions being received mentally.

What is the best time for that hour [of meditation]?

Either 11 to 12 in the day or 11 to 12 in the evening, or the best time is 2 to 3 in the morning! (262-100)

Another person was told:

Turn about, and pray a little oftener...let a whole moon pass...28 days...and never fail to pray at two o'clock in the

173.

morning. Rise and pray—facing east! You will be surprised at how much peace and harmony will come into thy soul. (3509-1)

The eastward-facing orientation, recommended in the preceding excerpt, should be carefully noted. It is consistent with what one finds in many teachings on the subject of meditation, as well as the Cayce readings.

Cayce's "Search for God" Study Group once asked:

For how long should this hour meditation be observed?
Each in their own way, but at least thirty minutes or the hour.
For how long at a period?
How long has it been given? Six months or a year? How long does it become necesssary? Some will want to continue, some will be through in a few days; for it will be as the sower giveth forth to sow. (262-101)

The length of the meditation will vary with the seeker. Five minutes is probably long enough at first, at least for some. This should be increased gradually as the person can quiet his mind and body for longer intervals.

Through the *thorough* application of *mind* over the existent condition, and with the application of that that will assist, both physical and mental, in bringing that condition about, from a physical viewpoint. That is, by this constant entering in, at a specific time, the quietude of self, or into the silence with self, for at least—beginning first for five to ten minutes, increasing this, day by day, a few minutes, until at least *thirty* minutes may be spent in such. (4329-1)

Where shall this body take this solitude, when concentrating?

174.

Any place the body may choose, being alone, and in the same place each day.   (137-3)

3. Position. Some religious philosophies or teachings put emphasis on posture, or position, during the practice of meditation. Yogis sit cross-legged with ankles locked on their thighs. This position is, however, either very uncomfortable or impossible for many Westerners. One must be relaxed; and any position which is comfortable may normally be assumed, just as long as the spine is not curved but held erect (supported in a straight position.) You many stand, sit, or even lie down; but, if lying down, cross the hands over the solar plexus.

What is the proper posture for my meditation?
As has been indicated before, each individual is an entity, each individual has had and is—not a law unto itself, but—a development unto the LAW!
That then becomes rather that which is to the entity the more expressive of that being sought to be attained in the experience. Thus as the entity has attained, as the entity has gained in itself, at times the pose or posture would be different. As these vary, meet same.   (903-24)

In what position may I best meditate?
As has been given, there are given to each their own respective manners, from their varied experiences, as to *how*, as to form. If *form* becomes that that is the guiding element, then the hope or the faith is lost in form! He that made long prayer, or he that not even raised his eyes but smote his breast and said, 'God be merciful to me, a sinner!' *Who* was justified? He that in humbleness of self, humbleness of mind, humbleness of the whole *individuality (losing* personality in Him) comes; and in *whatsoever* manner that—whether prone, whether standing, whether walking, or whether sleeping—we live, we die, in the Lord.   (262-17)

Yet, certain aspects of "form," if not carried to an extreme, do seem to be recommended in the readings, generally, as aids to our better attunement. Facing east, as mentioned earlier, was given as the best polarity during meditation:

> [What is the best polarity for this body] as it meditates?
> Facing the East, to be sure. (2072-12)

4. Mental and Physical Preparation. When you have chosen a time and place for your daily communing with God, through meditation, prepare yourself mentally and physically for this period of "entering into the silence."

There are many aides to this preparation and the readings made various suggestions, which are reviewed briefly. Try these and use whatever may seem helpful to you.

Reading the Bible or some other inspirational material puts the mind in a spiritually receptive mood. Maybe the Lord's Prayer is all that is necessary for you. Listening to certain kinds of music, such as the harp or flute or various stringed instruments, is perhaps the most helpful approach. The vibrations of music, softly played—if it is the right kind—can have a decidedly soothing effect, which elevates and stills the mind and relaxes the body. Such things as odors, flowers, soft (white) lights, incense, certain stones or crystals worn on the body or held in the hand, and so on may be of special help. They do set the mood, thereby aiding the beginner or even the experienced meditator.

5. Fasting. Physical fasting, according to one's own concept of same, may be very beneficial to some. It does cleanse and prepare the physical body. However, we have already noted that the Edgar Cayce readings define "true" fasting as focusing on a spiritual ideal and purpose, and abstaining from negative emotions or attitudes in our relationships with others.

6. Cleansing. The necessity of cleansing the physical surroundings was emphasized by the Cayce readings. It is a symbolic form of purification. Certainly a clean or chaste environment provides a more spiritual setting for the act of meditation.

Even more important, obviously, is the cleansing of the mind. No one can listen to God, or serve as an effective channel for His blessings to pour forth to ourselves and others, if the mind is cluttered with unclean thoughts or other mental obstructions.

> First, cleanse the room; cleanse the body; cleanse the surroundings, in thought, in act! Approach not the inner man, or the inner self, with a grudge or an unkind thought held against *any* man or do so to thine own undoing sooner or later! (281-13)

> In whatever manner that to thine own consciousness is a cleansing of the body and of the mind, that ye may present thyself *clean* before thyself and before thy God, *do!* Whether washing of the body with water, purging of same with oils, or surrounding same with music or incense. But *do that thy consciousness* directs thee! No questioning! For he that doubteth has already built his barrier. (826-11)

> For that we think on, as what we assimilate in our bodies, that we gradually grow to be. (1562-1)

The preparation and cleansing are always an individual matter:

> Whatever manner of cleansing, physical, mental or spiritual, that seems necessary, that *do;* consistently; not because any other one person or individual merely suggests same. But prepare thy mind and body as if ye would meet thy Lord and Master! Then sit as in readiness, at designated periods. Talk with Him from thine inner self,

as though He were physically present; for mentally and spiritually He *is* ever present. For, He has given, 'Lo, I am with thee always; I stand at the door and knock.' This is not merely a saying. Keep the awareness consciously of that visitation—by keeping that tryst with thy inner self and thy Lord consistently.   (1152-9)

It becomes necessary for each individual through some *particular* form, some particular activity, to reach an awareness or a consciousness. It is necessary that every individual withdraw; consecrating, purifying the body, the mind. But that each should withdraw at some given hour, or that each should sit in some individual form, or each should repose in some particular angle, or each should bathe in some particular water, or each should use some particular odor, or each should have some particular *thought* upon entering—this is *confusion*, see?   (993-4)

7. Head and Neck Exercises. This series of exercises for the head and neck is recommended as a useful preliminary to meditation. While performing these exercises, keep the body erect, moving only the head and neck as indicated.

1. Tilt head directly forward as far as it will go; return to erect position. Repeat three times, in a normal, rhythmic movement.

2. Drop head back as far as it will go; return to normal position. Repeat three times.

3. Tilt head to right side as far as it will go; return to original position. Repeat three times.

4. Tilt head to left side, and return to original position. Repeat three times.

5. In a circular movement, clockwise, drop head forward and rotate in a tilted position back to starting point. Repeat three times.

6. Do same as (5), above, in a counter-clockwise direction. Repeat three times.

8. Breathing. Only simple breathing exercises are recommended, for Edgar Cayce warned:

> For, breath is the basis of the living organism's activity. Thus such exercises may be beneficial or detrimental in their effect upon a body.
>
> Hence it is necessary that an understanding be had as to how, as to when, or in what manner such may be used.
>
> (2475-1)

> The raising of the life force may be brought about by certain characters of breathing—for, as indicated, the breath is power in itself; and this power may be directed to certain portions of the body. But for what purpose?   (2475-1)

A summary of the breathing exercise used by the Prayer Group is given here. The phrases were suggested by one of the group members to keep one in a devotional attitude, although the alternate breathing instructions were given in trance-state by Mr. Cayce. Use this formula if you find it helpful. The words can be spoken aloud or used silently as you prefer.

1. Breathe in through the right nostril and out through the mouth; repeat three times. (The left nostril should be closed.) Preceding each inhalation, say:

   a) (First breath): In the Name of the Father;
   b) (Second breath): In the Name of the Son;
   c) (Third breath): In the Name of the Holy Ghost.

2. Now breathe in through the left nostril, emiting breath through the right nostril. (Close right nostril while breathing in, then close left nostril while breathing out through right.) Repeat three times. Preceding each inhalation, say:

   a) (First breath): To the glory of God;
   b) (Second breath): To the glory of the Son;
   c) (Third breath): To the glory of the Holy Ghost.

The breathing exercises stimulate the nerves along the spine. Breathing through the right nostril affects the physical body while breathing through the left nostril affects the spiritual self. This alternate breathing exercise should not be performed hurriedly. It is well to breathe in on a count of seven, hold the breath for a count of three, and then exhale. This establishes the right rhythm.

The Prayer Group was told:

In breathing, take into the right nostril, STRENGTH! Exhale through thy mouth. Intake in thy left nostril, exhaling through the right; opening the centers of thy body — if it is first prepared to thine *own* understanding, thine *own* concept of what *ye* would have if ye would have a visitor, if ye would have a companion, if ye would have thy bridegroom!

Then, as ye begin with incantation of the Ar-ar-r-r-r — the e-e-e, the o-o-o, the m-m-m, *raise* these in thyself; and ye become close in the presence of thy Maker — as is *shown* in thyself! They that do such for selfiish motives do so to their own undoing. Thus has it oft been said, the fear of the Lord is the beginning of wisdom.

Wisdom, then, is fear to misapply knowledge in thy dealings with thyself, thy fellow man.   (281-28)

9. *Chanting.* Chanting, the third exercise, is done to stimulate the head centers — the pineal and pituitary glands, and their etheric counterparts. It may be omitted if music is used or if one's surroundings do not permit the use of this audible phase of the meditation process. Many, however, find it very helpful.

Throughout the ages man has used sound as a means of stimulation and motivation, of a spiritual nature or otherwise. There is the Mohammedan call to prayer and the uniquely Christian sound of the church bells calling to worship. And in Hinduism and Buddhism, there is the mantra. Also, at quite another level in the use of sound to rouse certain emotions or energies, there is the Indian war cry, the beat of the tom-toms and the frenzied war dance; though these may be said to represent negative uses of sound, of course. Similarly, the various African tribes have used drums for all types of tribal communication.

Here, then, is a brief version of the directions given for meditative chanting: Ar-ar-rr, E-e-e-e, O-o-o, M-m-m.

The readings state that this should be sung in the scale from C to C. Or it may also be sung in a monotone. The sounds are repeated three or seven times.

Another chant is OHM, or AUM. This may be chanted three to seven times.

Finally, a third form of chanting involves the sound, "Amen," which may be sung seven times.

The directions given to the Prayer Group at various times were these:

Seek then in tone—all of you—Ar-r-r-r-r-AR, that ye may know how the emanations, that are termed as the colors of the body, make for the expression then given.

With the music came then the dance, that enabled those with the disturbing forces and influences to become more erect, upright in body, in thought, in activity.   (281-25)

In the next reading, inquiry was made as to the key for this chant. The answer given:

It is the *combination*, or a treble from C to C.   (281-26)

The following examples indicate that chanting may be a very individual preparation or experience, which is influenced by former earth-lives.

As to the manner of meditation, then: Begin with that which is Oriental in its nature—Oriental incense. Let the mind become, as it were, attuned to such by the humming, producing those sounds of O-o-o-ah-ah-umm-o-o-; not as to become monotonous, but "feel" the essence of the incense through the body-forces in its motion of body. Surround self ever with that purpose, 'Not my will, O God, but Thine be done, ever'—and the entity will gain vision, perception, and, most of all, judgment. (2823-3)

For, as has been indicated from the innate experience as well as from the longings within, a home—*home*—with all its deeper, inner meanings, is a portion of the entity's desire; to know, to experience, to have the 'feel' of, to have the surroundings of that implied by the word *home!* Is it any wonder then that in all of thy meditation, Ohm-O-h-m-mmm has ever been, is ever a portion of that which raises self to the highest influence and the highest vibrations throughout its whole being that may be experienced by the entity? (1286-1)

With the return (of the priest Ra Ta from exile), and with the healing of the body for the greater activities, the entity arose in its thought and power through its application especially in the Temple Beautiful.

And from same comes that interest in harmony, and color—as does the sounding of that as was the call from the station of the third position in the Temple Beautiful over which the entity, as Omuna, presided—sound within self—O-oooo-ah-m-mmm-u-uuu-u-uuu-n-nnn. These as they may be sounded within; not just the vocal box of the physical but as they rise along the centers from the bodily forces to unite the activities—the entity may bring greater harmony within the experience, as it did to many through the activities in that material sojourn. (1770-2)

Any specific compositions that can be used for healing?
R and O and M are those combinations which vibrate to the center forces of the body itself. In any compositions of

which these are a part there will be found that necessary for the individual. What might be healing for one might be distracting for another, to be sure. (1861-12)

10. Protection. Before moving from the preparatory stages into the actual meditation, it is important to surround oneself with the protective powers of those creative forces with which attunement is being sought. In this regard, one man was told:

Never open self, my friend, without surrounding self with the spirit of the Christ, that ye may ever be guarded and guided by His forces! (440-8)

An affirmation of protection was offered in another reading:

I surround, I claim, the presence of the Christ; that there may be the more perfect understanding, the more perfect accord as one with the purpose of my experience—now. (585-4)

Surrounding self with the light of the Christ Consciousness was the way this reading phrased it, as a protection against "the dark influence":

How may I bring about greater emotional stability?
Surround self with the light of the Christ Consciousness, by thought, by word of mouth, by impressing it upon self. And in that light there may never [be] any harm to self or... self being entertained or used by the dark influence. (2329-3)

Finally, here is a beautiful protective prayer, or affirmation, recommended to one individual as a prelude to meditation:

As I surround myself with the consciousness of the

Christ-Mind, may I—in body, in purpose, in desire—be purified to become the channel through which He may DIRECT me in that He, the Christ, would have me do.

(1947-3)

When you pray for protection, it may be helpful to visualize yourself in the center of light. Imagine the purest, whitest light possible and visualize yourself completely surrounded by it. This is the Christ Light, and nothing can harm you when you do this. This light and your protective prayer will guard and protect you any time you are in need, whether or not you are meditating. It is a protective, healing force.

11. *Affirmation*. Your preparations made, you are now ready to be still and focus on the affirmation that will be your "centering point" in the meditation itself. The Edgar Cayce method is to focus on an affirmation or short prayer. Many Westerners, in approaching meditation, use only the Lord's Prayer as a focal point. Some students of meditation are taught to concentrate on a flower, a seed, a specific mantram, a mandala, the so-called "third-eye," or their breathing. But whatever you select for the focusing of your attention, you will be confronted with the same necessity of finding the right catalyst to break free from external distractions and "enter into the silence." This is the meditative state.

The affirmation has the advantage of providing a "seed thought" on which to focus, while its content feeds the subconscious mind and the inner being.

In thinking about the seed thought, try to rise above the intellectual analysis and intuitively understand the meaning and experience the power of the idea. Then, simply fix your attention upon the chosen affirmation; let your mind focus upon it—but remain a detached observer in this process, rather than engaging the conscious mind in active thought about it. For, such mental activity will block the transition to an altered state of consciousness, which meditation is all about. You will then be unable to enter the silence, and listen to the still, small voice within.

Here, as an illustration, is an affirmation we might consider:

> Lord, Thou art my dwelling place. Let Thy *will*, Thy purpose, fill my mind, my body, that *my* will may be one with Thee. (281-26)

Though relatively brief, this might be reduced to its essence—"Thy will, Thy purpose, Lord"; or, "THY will *my* will"—which will aid in concentration. It then becomes like a Zen aphorism, pithy and succinct. See this mental expression or image in your mind's eye—don't *think* about it, *see* it—until you have become a completely detached observer. If you are not apt at visualizing a mental concept in this manner, then you may wish to repeat the words over and over, until the focus is established at both the conscious and unconscious levels.

Concentrated attention on the affirmation is difficult to maintain at first. Do not let this fact disturb you. In time, with practice, you will learn the process. Remember, as quoted earlier, one must *learn* meditation, like learning to walk, to talk.

Considered from the standpoint of reincarnation, we can see how it sometimes happens that one individual acquires the art of meditation much faster than another, having mastered this discipline in a prior life, or even in several lives. Normally speaking, however, the Occidental has not been programmed to meditative techniques, but is conditioned to limiting his approach to God in terms of Christian prayer. Prayer is vital, of course. Edgar Cayce consistently emphasized the need for prayer. But he also emphasized that "stepped up" version of prayer, which is meditation. It is a form of prayer at a higher, more direct level of approach to the Godhead.

Prayer can be effective *before* meditation as a means of conditioning the mind for spiritual attunement to follow; but *after* meditation, our prayer is imbued with greater healing power and effectiveness, particularly if we had attained that state of altered consciousness that comes with training, and in deeper, longer periods of meditation. Then, through our prayers, we are able to send forth healing vibrations to others. And, "Healing others is healing self," said Cayce in reading 281-18.

Moreover, the readings quite definitely state that the raising of creative energies in meditation *must* be directed outward, in service to others through prayer and healing work or some other expression, such as lecturing or teaching, or activity in one of the creative arts that enables us to communicate the messages of the Higher Self to others.

12. *General Preparation.* When an individual then enters into deep meditation:

It has been found throughout the ages that self-preparation *is* necessary. To some it is necessary that the body be cleansed with pure water, that certain types of breathing are taken, that there may be an even balance in the whole of the respiratory system, that the circulation becomes normal in its flow throught the body, that certain or definite odors produce those conditions that allay or stimulate the activity of portions of the system, that the more carnal or more material sources are laid aside, or the whole body is *purified* so that the purity of thought as it rises has less to work against in its dissemination of that it brings to the whole of the system, in its rising through the whole of these centers, stations or places along the body.
(281-13)

Then, as one formula—not the only one, to be sure—for an individual that would enter into meditation for self, for others:

Cleanse the body with pure water. Sit or lie in an easy position, without binding garments about the body. Breathe in through the right nostril three times, and exhale through the mouth. Breathe in three times through the left nostril and exhale through the right.

Then, either with the aid of a low music, or the incantating of that which carries self deeper—deeper—to the seeing, feeling, experiencing of that image in the creative forces of love, enter into the Holy of Holies. As self feels or experiences the raising of this, see it disseminated through the inner eye (not the carnal eye) to that which will bring the greater understanding in meeting every condition in the experience of the body.

Then listen to the music that is made as each center of thine own body responds to that new creative force that is being, and that is disseminated through its own channel; and we will find that little by little this entering in will enable self to renew all that is necessary—in Him. (281-13)

Affirmations

From the Edgar Cayce readings, here is a helpful selection of affirmations or prayers that may be used for healing meditation:

There is being raised within me that Christ Consciousness that is sufficient for every need within my body, my mind, my soul. (281-7)

May that strength as was manifest in the consciousness of the Christ life be so magnified in me as to make every atom of my body conscious of His presence working in and through me, bringing that to pass as He sees I have need of now. (281-12)

Create within me a pure heart, O God, and renew a righteous spirit within me, that thy love may bring that thou seest is best for me now. (281-5)

There is being created in my body that divine love of the

Christ consciousness, that will eradicate all uncommon, or any desires that would hinder the body from being physically fit. (281-5)

Our God, our Father, let my desires and the meditations of my heart, of my body, of my mind, be ONE with Thee that I may be renewed and made every whit whole.
(281-26)

I surround, I claim, the presence of the Christ; that there may be the more perfect understanding, the more perfect accord as one with the purpose of my experience—now.
(585-4)

The Father that worketh in me supplieth the needs of the body, of the mind, of the soul, even as I work His ways!
(281-22)

Create in me, O Father, that peace, that harmony, that love, that will bring the comprehension of thy love, thy mercy, thy grace, in me, in my being just now. (281-17)

Father, let thy love, thy mercy, thy truth in the Christ sustain me and keep me in the way I should go! (281-22)

The Healing Light

The Edgar Cayce readings, particularly the Prayer Group series, offer extensive direction and guidance for meditation. Only a portion of that material has been excerpted in this book; there is a great deal more that the earnest seeker will find worth pursuing. Of outstanding note in the readings is the synonymity between the Light, or the healing principle, and the Christ presence:

What is Light? That from which, through which, in which may be found all things out of which all things come. Thus the first of everything which may be visible in earth, in heaven and in space is of that Light, is that Light. (2533-8)

Find that light in self. It isn't the light of the noonday sun, nor the moon, but rather of the Son of man. (3491-1)

For He is the LIGHT; He IS Light, and in Him is no darkness at all! (262-115)

Light *is*. It is all about us at all times, unhindered by the dimensions of time or space, but we must attune to it to experience it. We can use it and direct it (or, more accurately, let *it* use and direct *us*), even if we do not "see" it. However, with continued meditation and application, we *do* come to see this Christ Light with the mind's eye, or inner eye—"the single eye of service," as reading 281-27 calls it.

We can erase, dissolve or transmute any condition or problem by simply releasing our hold on it and turning it over to God, letting Him take care of the situation in His own way.

Here are some excerpts from the readings which were published under the title "Let There Be Light" and used by the original A.R.E. Prayer Group in their healing activities:

Early in the morning call unto thy God, and in the evening forget not His love nor His benefits.

Then, at that period when ye are first aware, as ye awake, be STILL a moment and know that the Lord is God. Ask that ye be guided, THIS day, to so live that ye may stand between the living and the dead.

In the evening as ye sit at meat, be STILL a moment; for there is greater power in being still before thy God than in much speaking. Again give thanks for the day and its opportunities. (281-60)

He has promised to take our burdens upon Himself, so

189.

let our prayers be: 'I CANNOT BEAR THIS ALONE, MY SAVIOR, MY CHRIST, I SEEK THY AID.'

And such a cry has never, no never, been denied the believing and acting heart.

'Lord, here I am! Use me in the way, in the manner Thou seest fit; that I may ever be that Thou hast purposed for me to be, a light shining in darkness to those who have lost hope from one cause or another. (3976-26)

Finally, here is a suggested "Meditation on the Light" for healing or dissolving any problem:

1. *I release all of my past to God.*
   Saying that you release all of your past is a positive statement which reaches the subconscious and helps you to let go of the past. It also helps you to forgive yourself. Remember, God always forgives; but first you must forgive yourself!
2. *I release all of my negative thoughts to God.*
   This is a form of repentance, turning over to God all negative or destructive thought patterns you have built and accumulated. In letting them go, you are automatically asking for and receiving God's forgiveness.
3. *I release all of my fears to God.*
   Your fears may be one of your greatest problems. If this is so, they are a big part of your karma.

For being afraid is the first consciousness of sin's entering in, for he that is afraid has lost consciousness of self's own heritage. (243-10)

Fear is as the fruit of indecisions respecting that which is lived and that which is held as the ideal. Doubt is as the father of fear. Remember, as He gave, 'He that asks in my name, doubting not, shall have; for I go to the Father.'

Fear is as the beginning of faltering. Faltering is as that which makes for dis-ease throughout the soul and the mental body. (538-33)

Self-awareness, *selfishness*, is that which makes men afraid. The awareness of the necessities of the carnal forces in a material world seeking their gratification.

(262-29)

'Perfect love casteth out fear.' (136-18)

4. *I release all human relationships to God.*
   You are turning over to God your human emotions and entanglements, the entire gamut of your inter-personal relationships, so that he may direct them in purposeful and constructive paths.
5. *I release myself, my inner self, to God.*
   Here you are reaching up to God, so that He may reach down to you.

Now see yourself being FILLED WITH LIGHT, and say:
   1. I replace all my past with Light.
   2. I replace all my negative thoughts with Light.
   3. I replace all my fears with Light.
   4. I replace all human relationships with Light.
   5. I radiate Light in every atom of my being.
   6. I am filled with Light from within and without.
   7. I am surrounded by Light.

Now sit quietly and visualize this Light, knowing that it is the Christ presence. *See* it, inwardly; *feel* it. Know that your body is *filled* with it. With the mind's eye, or inner eye, let this Light focus on any troubled spot within your body—knowing that the body is indeed the temple of the soul, and can be made a channel for Light in every atom, every cell.

Hold yourself in this cleansing Light. Thank God for It. Then say:

I am a light being. I radiate light to everything and everybody. Thank you, God, for everything!

AFTERWORD

The Biochemical Basis of Karma

by Michael James, Ph.D.

The efforts of pioneering physicians have led to a new age of medical treatment. Termed holistic medicine, the practitioners of this healing art aid the patient in harmonizing the three essential aspects of his being: spirit, mind and body.

Holistic medicine treats spirit and the physical body as two ends of the same continuum, with body given form by mind. Thus, the cause of disease is found in spirit while the effect is in a physical vehicle mediated by mind. In an effort to span the knowledge gap between the spiritual and biochemical aspects of the healing arts, I present a hypothesis which is consistent with the current theories of medical science. It is not my intention to prove with scientific rigor the theory which will be put forth. Rather, my purpose is to provide encouragement for those whose faith may have faltered.

For there is the law of the material, there is the law of the mental, there is the law of the spiritual. That which is brought into materiality is first conceived in spirit. (3395-2)

Since the physical woes of each individual are generated by our misuse of spiritual force, all healing must ultimately come from spirit. This is done by attuning self to a healing vibration; that is, a vibration that is constructive in its very essence. Constructive vibrations can be realized through desire and application. The purpose and the ideal of the individual determine the vibration to which the self is attuned. The daily application of one's ideal will ensure that the same vibration is held. To be sure, healing with spiritual force represents the greatest challenge. Once this is accomplished, bodily healing is the inevitable result, although it may be aided in part by external stimuli.

And if thy life is disturbed, if thy heart is sad, if thy body is racked with pain, it is thine bungling of the laws that are as universal as Life itself. (281-27)

Before any attempt at physical healing is undertaken, the contents of the mind should be examined. All mental barriers to good health must be eliminated. The desire to be healthy will not become manifest as long as the personal conscious beliefs prevent it. These conscious beliefs can be carried from lifetime to lifetime, resulting in the same maladies being perpetuated from one incarnation to the next. For example, the sufferer may choose to be ill in order to command the attention and sympathy of those who are close to him. Or an illness may be a means of inflicting punishment on oneself to atone for past actions that the entity recognizes at the unconscious level to have been "improper" in respect to its established standards of conduct, morally speaking. Or the malady may reflect the result of one's ingrained belief in the incompatibility of good health with a spiritually-evolved nature.

Indeed, there are as many belief systems as there are individuals. The point at which to begin is the present. We must set aside some introspective moments for examining our individual belief system, if we suffer from a persistent illness, and surrender those beliefs which may be hindering our recovery.

For the environs and the hereditary influences are spiritual as well as physical, and are physical because of the spiritual application of the abilities of the entity in relationship to spiritual development.   (852-12)

The physical man is, in part, a product of both nature and nurture. The hereditary influences provide man with his nature (or biological potentials and limitations) while the environment provides the nurture. The interaction of man's hereditary and environmental factors gives man his distinctive anatomical, biochemical, physiological and behavioral characteristics. At first glance, it appears that the environmental and hereditary factors cannot be altered. Yet the Edgar Cayce readings have given that:

There is no urge in the astrological, in the vocational, in the hereditary or environmental which surpasses the will or determination of the entity.   (5023-2)

How, then, can the will or determination be used to correct any hereditary disorders? Before this question can be answered, it will be necessary to review briefly the science of genetics.

Genetics is that branch of biology concerned with heredity and variation. The hereditary units which are transmitted from one generation to the next (inherited) are called genes. The genes are a particular sequence of subunits arranged along a molecule called deoxyribonucleic acid (DNA). The DNA, in conjunction with a protein matrix, is organized into structures called chromosomes, which are found in the nucleus of the cell. The genes of the living cell contain all the information needed for the cell to reproduce itself. Genes bear, in coded form, the detailed specifications for the thousands of kinds of protein molecules the cell requires for its moment-to-moment existence. Thus, the activities of life in the living cell proceed under the direction of the genes. Conglomerations of cells give rise to tissues and organs which perform their roles through the co-operative effort of their cells.

The control of tissue and organ function has been under scientific investigation for more than a century. Gradually it has become clear that among the primary controllers are the endocrine hormones. Thus, the genes control the activities of individual cells which constitute the tissues and organs that respond to the influence of the hormones. Genes do not operate continuously but are switched on and off. It has been found that the pattern of genetic activity in responsive cells is rapidly altered by the endocrine hormones. It is also known that in any chromosome a substantial amount of DNA does not exhibit genetic activity.

Considering my ideals, purposes and karmic pattern, as well as the conditions which I face at present, in what specific direction should I seek expression for my talents and abilities in order to render the greatest possible service?

This is rather a compound question, for it presumes or presupposes as to ideals, as to purposes, and as to self's concept of karma.

What *is* karma? and what *is* the pattern?

He alone is each soul pattern. He *alone* is each soul pattern! *He* is thy *karma,* if ye put thy trust *wholly* in Him! See? (2067-2)

The living flesh is the material manifestation of the soul, and I propose that the individual soul pattern is encoded in the DNA of the cellular chromosomes. DNA which exhibits genetic activity represents the karmic pattern into which the soul incarnates. DNA which does *not* exhibit genetic activity represents the potential within each individual. Since He (the Christ) *is* each soul pattern, and since He is our karma, the chromosomes contain what could be termed "Christ genes,"

196.

which are dormant, waiting to be awakened, presumably. If they could be activated, these "Christ genes" would give rise to a healthy physical body since they would exert their regenerative effects at the cellular level.

> Yet it is found that within the body there are channels, there are ducts, there are glands, there are activities that perform no one knows what in a living, *moving*, thinking being. (281-41)

> *Meditation* properly done must make one *stronger* mentally, physically.
> As has been given, there are *definite* conditions that arise from within the inner man when an individual enters into true or deep meditation. A physical condition happens, a physical activity takes place! (281-13)

The preceding excerpts from the Edgar Cayce readings refer, of course, to the endocrine system and suggest that the endocrine glands may be activated in meditation. Such activation, we may conclude, will alter the body's hormone levels, which should affect genetic expression. If genetic expression can indeed be modified through the daily practice of meditation, it should thereby be possible to selectively activate the "Christ genes," according to our ideal. It should be understood, however, that meditation must be approached *intelligently*. The person who meditates without proper safeguards or purpose often induces a wide range of physical difficulties, because he is focusing intense energy into an untrained physical system. Meditation *ought* to generate good physical health, but approached naively, it can lead to physical problems.

> For know first, the image must be in the spiritual ideal before it may become a factor in the mental self for material expression. (1440-2)

The ideal which is held in meditation should define the precise hormone levels which are realized as a result of the meditation. Theoretically, a selfless spiritual ideal held in meditation should give rise to the hormonal balance which will activate the "Christ genes." If this is done consistently, a healthy physical body should, in due time, become manifest.

About the author: Michael James is the pen name of a Ph.D. research scientist who is affiliated with a major cancer research center in the United States.

RECOMMENDED READING

Alibrandi, Tom. *The Meditation Handbook,* Major Books, 1976.

Bailey, Herbert. *GH3: Will It Keep You Young Longer?,* Bantam Books, 1977.

Cheraskin, Dr. E., & Ringsdorf, W.M. Jr., with Brecher, Arline. *Psycho-Dietetics,* Bantam Books, 1974.

Fere, Dr. Maud Tresillian. *Does Diet Cure Cancer?,* Thorsons (England), 1971.

Finkel, Maurice. *Fresh Hope in Cancer,* Billings & Stone Ltd. (England), 1978.

Furst, Jeffrey. *Edgar Cayce's Story of Attitudes and Emotions,* Berkeley, 1972.

Griffin, G. Edward. *World Without Cancer,* American Media, 1974.

Jensen, Bernard. *Health Magic Through Chlorophyll,* Jensen's Nutritional & Health Producers, 1976.

Joy, W. Brugh, M.D. *Joy's Way,* J.P. Tarcher, 1979.

Leichtman, Dr. Robert R. & Japikse, Carl. *Active Meditation: The Western Tradition,* Ariel Press, 1982.

Leichtman, Dr. Robert R. & Japikse, Carl. *The Way To Health*, Ariel Press, 1979.

Leitner, Stanley A. *Last Chance to Live*, Wade Allen, 1979.

Netherton, Morris, & Shiffrin, Nancy. *Past Life Therapy*, Ace Books, 1979.

Parker, William R. *Prayer Therapy*, William R. Parker, 1969.

Soyka, Fred, with Edmonds, Alan. *The Ion Effect*, McClelland & Stewart-Bantam Ltd. (Canada), 1978.

Steadman, Alice, *Who's the Matter with Me?*, 1968.

Walker, N.W. *Raw Vegetable Juices*, Norwalk Press, 1970.

White Eagle. *Heal Thyself*, White Eagle Publishing Trust (England), 1962.

Woodward, Mary Ann. *Be Still and Know*, A.R.E. Press, 1962.

Woodward, Mary Ann. *Edgar Cayce's Story of Karma*, Berkeley, 1972.

Woodward, Mary Ann. *That Ye May Heal*, A.R.E. Press, 1970.